AND TO MY NEPHEW ALBERT

I leave the Island
what I won off
Fatty Hagan in a
poker game...

DAVID FORREST

AND TO
MY NEPHEW ALBERT

I leave the Island
what I won off
Fatty Hagan in a
poker game...

BOOK OF THE MONTH CLUB

Copyright © 1969 by David Forrest

First printed 1969

This edition published in 1969
by arrangement with Hodder & Stoughton Limited
by The Book of the Month Club Limited
4 Fitzroy Square, London W1

Printed in Great Britain by
Willmer Brothers Limited, Birkenhead

Draw a line due south from the Bishop Rock lighthouse, on the Scilly Isles. And a second line, south by a quarter west from Penninis Head on St Mary's. Where the two intersect, some seventeen miles away, and about eighty-five miles off the most westerly corner of France, there is a boat...

1 "D'you get whales round here?"

"Not often," replied the boatman.

"Well, I think I can see one straight ahead," said Albert. He peered through his binoculars at the black shape, just showing above the waves on the horizon.

"Here, 'ave a look."

The boatman balanced himself so that he was holding the wheel steady with the weight of his chest against it. He focused Albert's binoculars.

"Whale, me darlin'? That's yer bloody rock."

Albert almost snatched the binoculars back.

"Where's the trees, then?"

"Trees, me darlin'? Yer couldn't grow old there, let alone grass't 'un such."

The rock became larger, starker and uglier.

"I thought all the Scilly Isles had trees and flowers," persisted Albert. He refused to believe his legacy island was barren.

"I 'spect they was there once," said the boatman. "They probably fell off the first time the wind blowed."

"Are you sure that this is Foul Rock? You couldn't have made a mistake?"

The boatman smiled. "Been coming out here a long time, son. There's only one Foul Rock around here—and that's it."

He manoeuvred the launch into a small cove on the western end of the island. From close up, it looked even bleaker. It was interesting only near the water's edge where seaweed hung over the salt-whitened rocks.

"I can't get right inshore. Have to jump. Pick a clean rock or that kelp'll tip yer into the 'oggin. I'll be back to

7

pick yer up at about four this afternoon... By the way," the boatman became suddenly concerned. "Don't go swimmin', or nothin' like that on yer own. I'd hate to lose a payin' customer."

"See you," shouted Albert, as he jumped ashore. "Don't bloody well forget me, will you?"

It was a hot June day. The sea was gently rattling the pebbles at the water's edge as the boat reversed away.

"Those crummy travel brochures," thought Albert as he began his hike across his kingdom. "Come to the Scilly Isles. Palm trees, long sandy beaches, flowers. Castles an' greenhouses. Botanical gardens. Swimmin' pools an' lagoons. And what do I get? A bleedin' quarry. Not even a dandelion." He was suddenly surprised to find himself half-way along the Island. He had taken just seventy-five paces. He looked around him. He was standing on the highest point, a smooth plateau twenty feet above the high-tide mark. He could have thrown a stone into the sea in any direction. It was only thirty-seven and a half yards to his left and right. And another seventy-five yards ahead.

"Flaming 'ell," he said quietly. "Not a grovelling peasant in sight."

A movement on a small rock a few yards out in the rippled sea caught his eye.

"Me loyal subjects."

He examined them. They examined back. A pair of cormorants watched him like vultures. A tatty herring-gull, with a distinctive limp, eyed him with apprehension from a shrivelled clump of seaweed.

Albert swept them a regal bow.

"Me Lord, Lady and Gen'leman, your king is abdicating."

One look was enough. He made up his mind to return to St Mary's. But, by the time he'd picked his way back to the beach, through the rocky crevices, he found the boatman was well out of calling range. He could just see the launch, a diminishing dot on the horizon. Albert cursed the arrangement he'd made. Now he was stuck on the rock until evening.

"Shit!" he said. He filled his lungs and shouted the

word, loudly. "SHH-II-TT!" The two cormorants swirled into the air in panic, collided and collapsed in a tangled heap into the sea. The dilapidated gull took two drunken limps while watching him over its shoulder, and stunned itself on a rocky outcrop.

"Take the day off," Albert decreed. "Albert the First's having a Royal shufty."

The King pushed his hands into the back pockets of his jeans and booted a large pebble into the water. He resumed his slow tour of his domain. "What a slagheap," he thought. It was then that he spotted the power-boat, a blue dart tugging at its moorings in the calm water of a cove. He started towards it.

" 'Ello," said Albert. "Somebody's towing me island away. Bit of a bloody sauce. Pirates. I just got 'ere in time. Call out the guard. KERR-RIST!"

A long, brown girl was lying twenty yards away against a wave-planed rock; so brown she was almost perfectly camouflaged alongside the kelp that hung in broad ribbons near the waterline. She glistened where the sunlight mirrored off the sea onto her oiled body.

She was sleek. Slim waisted and slim thighed. Her blonde hair was caught in a pony tail. She was nude— very. She lay back, her head pillowed in her hands. Her breasts, girlish and rounded, were as richly-tanned as the rest of her.

Albert looked. She was alone. As a collector of girls, he realised that this one was a desirable specimen. He thumbed through a mental catalogue.

"Vintage: about seventeen. October, probably. Moneyed, 'cos of the boat. High school—no, boarding school. Local girl, or unemployed, judging by grade of tan. Height: about five feet five inches. Weight: 105 lbs. I'd say 34-22-34. Natural blonde—so eyes blue or grey. Novice smoker. Arty, drinks halves of bitter."

"Boy friends? Unlikely—as brown all over, and obviously spends a lot of time on her own. Reckons she's too good for the locals. And as it's early in the season, hasn't had much chance with holidaymakers this year. Probably only left school last September, so chances are she doesn't have any. Sexual experience limited."

9

He contemplated the interesting statistics. "I'm king here. I could have her. She's invaded me. I could make her my prisoner of war."

This seemed like a good line of thought to pursue. Did an invader become a prisoner of war if no war had been declared? Or was the girl merely an illegal immigrant whom he'd have to deport? Alternatively, she might be a migrant who wanted to settle in his kingdom. Albert decided the girl was a tourist—after all, small countries like his needed tourists to strengthen their economies.

Albert pictured himself in an impressive scarlet uniform with gold epaulettes, brass buttons and a large peaked hat. With his cap at an official angle he'd stroll over to the girl and demand her passport.

"Passport? No passport? Sorry, straight to the nick."

He'd leave her for a few days on bread and water. Then he'd have her brought into his apartments, bathed, and clothed in silks. He'd invite her to dinner with him. He knew this established film technique would work—she'd throw herself into his bed out of gratitude.

He stood up and walked over to the girl. As he neared her, she reached out and calmly draped herself with a large beach towel.

She gave no other sign of knowing he was there. Her eyes appeared to be shut.

Albert half lifted the binoculars hanging round his neck. For a moment he thought of using them to examine her with greater care, but the eyes might open and that would be embarrassing. After all, he was now only a few feet from her.

His shadow fell across her. She opened one eye. It was a startling blue. The second eye opened. Albert was relieved to see that it was the same colour.

"You're standing in my sun."

Albert moved nearer and sat next to her.

"And you're sitting on my Island," he said.

The girl stared at him.

"Why don't you go and put your head underwater while I get dressed. It'll only take me ten minutes."

Albert looked away for three, watching the sparkle of

the small waves as they bounced against the rocks. Behind him he could hear the rustle of the girl's clothing.

"I heard you shouting a few minutes ago," she said. "Was it your family motto? You can look now."

Albert looked. He wondered why the girl had bothered to put on a bikini—it was so brief. There was just enough to show it was yellow.

Her blonde hair was streaked where it was bleached by the sun. Her eyebrows were almost white. Her features were strikingly Nordic. She reminded him of the dolly princess advertising pre-formed uplift bras on the boardings at his local Tube station. He decided against asking her whether she machine-washed her bra ninety-six times. It surprised him that he'd even read the advertisement's text.

He was pleased to see he had been right about the colour of her eyes, and about her accent. Now he noticed, with satisfaction, that she wasn't wearing a ring.

Mentally, Albert seduced her.

Her soft voice brought him back to reality. "I've never seen you before. I've been sunbathing here for ages."

Albert pulled out a battered packet of cigarettes and offered one to the girl. "First visit," he said. "I've just inherited it, so I guess that makes me king."

"So sue me, your Majesty. You're welcome to the place. It's no use for anything except sunbathing."

"Typical colonialist. Take all you want out of a country, then pretend that it's not worth having when you're being thrown out."

"I'll bet you're rich," she said. "A socialist with a right-wing bank balance.'

"Wrong. This Island's all I've got. I work in a cinema. What do you do?"

"Nothing," she replied. "Daddy's a solicitor in St Mary's. I just live with him. And I come here on hot days. Where did you leave your boat? It's not very safe to moor on the western end of the Island."

"I swam here," said Albert. "I'm a famous long-distance swimmer. It's only thirty-four miles the round trip."

"You're a nut!"

11

Albert lit her cigarette and admitted that he was stuck on the island for the next few hours.

"I've got some sandwiches, and I'm hungry," said the girl. "If you'd like to get them from my boat, I'll share them with you. They're in a plastic box. By the way, what's your name?"

"I'm Albert," he said. "Albert Quinlan."

The girl giggled.

"What's so funny?"

"Nothing really," she said. "Except that I'm Victoria."

He rose to his feet and made his way down to the power-boat. Victoria watched his tall figure. He bent over and searched for the box under the mahogany thwarts. Then he straightened and flicked back his brown hair with a casual jerk of his head.

"Not bad," she thought. "About twenty-four. Moves well. Sexy hips. London accent. He's sharp. Big, doggy eyes. Super!"

Albert came back. "Boat's a beauty," he said. "Yours?"

"Daddy's."

They ate their sandwiches in silence.

Albert decided he was glad he'd missed the boatman.

He stripped off his shirt and lay back beside the girl. The sun pressed down, until the rock itself steamed at the edges, where the waves whispered.

"Who d'you get the Island from?"

"My old Uncle Alf. He brought me up. He won it in a poker game. When I was a kid, he used to tell me he'd won me in a poker game. My mother died of pneumonia. Uncle Alf was looking after me till Dad got back from the war. He never did."

Uncle Alf, Albert explained, was a hard-drinking railway ganger who had come over to England to help the IRA struggle. He'd developed such a great liking for English beer that he'd almost completely foresaken the cause that brought him.

He was always wild. Frequently drunk. But he was a man with a great heart. He threw away most of his money as if it was going to be devalued at any moment. But he'd always kept enough to ensure that Albert was well-fed and housed.

To the boy he became mother and father, and bad example. And Albert loved him.

Since Uncle Alf won the Island in a card game in O'Flaharty's Bar in the East End of London, he'd spent the last months of his life dreaming of retiring there to beachcombing.

When he died, Albert, as sole heir, inherited the Island and several hundred empty beer bottles—carefully stored in every available cupboard and outhouse.

"After all," Uncle Alf used to tell Albert. "A wallet of cash can be stolen, but who's going to thieve beer bottles at tuppence a time each?"

Albert cleared out the small house and sold the bottle collection back to the pub for £9.14.2d. He'd seen his uncle decently buried. Afterwards, at the wake, Fatty Hagan told him it was a good thing Alf was a Roman Catholic, as his alcohol-filled body would have exploded if he'd been cremated.

Albert saved hard for his summer holidays on his Island. And here he was. . . .

"I don't think there's much you could do with this place," Victoria observed. "It's a bit desolate. I'd hate to live here in winter."

"I could turn it into a bird sanctuary," said Albert, eyeing Victoria speculatively.

"You like birds?"

"Watch them all the time," said Albert, truthfully. He waved his army surplus binoculars. "I get real close to them with these. I can see every detail."

"Do you know their names?"

"I always find out the names of the ones I like."

"What are those, then?" She pointed at the cormorants.

"The fat one's Leslie, and the scraggy one's Desmond."

She laughed. "They're cormorants. What's that one?" The lame herring-gull was balancing on one leg on its rocky perch.

"It's a stork," said Albert. "It's name's Cedric."

Victoria giggled. "You're a fraud. You don't know anything about them."

"I'm learning."

The rocks gave little shade from the hot sun. Albert

found the reflected glare from the water uncomfortable. He climbed to a narrow cleft just above Victoria, where there was a low shadow. From here he could watch her without her knowing, and the more he looked at her, the more he found to interest him.

"Swim?" asked Victoria.

"In what? Haven't got my trunks."

"What about your underpants?"

"Don't be personal."

"I don't mind if you swim in them. You won't embarrass me."

He stripped down to his jockey shorts with the beer label design. Albert and Victoria swam for a while in the clear water, then went back and sat on their rock and dried in the sun.

"This is a damn sight better than Manny's Biograph," said Albert.

"What?"

"It's the dump where I work. I'm the assistant manager. If we had as many customers as moths the gov'nor would be a millionaire."

"It sounds ugh," said Victoria.

"It's more than ugh, but it gets me. The people are marvellous. They're mostly pensioners. D'you know, one old bird complained to me last week that a mouse had eaten her sandwich when she'd left it on the seat next to her. I told her she shouldn't bring her mice in with her. She was choked. I had to buy her a hamburger. It cost *me* money. And she'd got in on a free ticket!"

Victoria was giggling again.

"What does your boss say?"

"Manny? He's great." Albert told her about him.

Manny was Jewish. Manny was generous. He never complained when Albert gave the hordes of old age pensioners free seats. In winter, Albert would have the boilers stoked, just to keep his special patrons warm. They'd come to the Biograph every day and sit through each performance from mid-day until closing time. They brought their food with them. Mostly, the films were old and bad, so there were always enough seats for paying customers, but none came. Occasionally, there would be

14

a good film—but the ranks of pensioners crowded out the paying customers. Still, Manny wasn't worried. Maybe he wouldn't make a fortune. And if he and Albert didn't look after the old age pensioners, who would?

"'Ave a bit of gefuelltefische, Albert. Stop thinking about your Island. Your future's 'ere with me, in show business," Manny would say. Albert would straighten his bow tie and smooth down his second-hand tuxedo. Then he would stroll to the back of the stalls to watch his hero, Douglas Fairbanks—Senior. D.F. Junior's films were still way above Manny's financial budget.

"Time to go," said Victoria. Albert looked sad.

They drove the boat back to St Mary's and stopped Albert's returning fisherman only a few hundred yards outside the harbour.

In the small guesthouse near Buzza Mill, Albert sat on his bed and thought about the day's trip. The Island was still disappointing. Victoria, on the other hand, was most promising. His holiday, after all, could turn out to be good. There might even be a treasure ship amongst the sunken reefs around Foul Rock. . . .

Now, in Mrs Pengelly's Edwardian Villa, Albert stripped down and tried to shower. It was difficult. Mrs Pengelly's shower was simply a jug and water basin. Albert put the bowl on a towel on the floor, then carefully stepped in. He poured half the cold water from the jug over his head and soaped himself. The second pouring washed off most of the soap. A towel got rid of the rest.

He dressed, and walked down into Hugh Town to meet Victoria in the snug of The Fisherman's Inn. She was already there. Albert awarded himself another mark. Victoria was holding a half-pint of bitter in her small hand. He liked beer-drinking girls. There was something about them, even if it was only economy. With her was a comical, portly figure. It looked like a Dickensian caricature. She introduced it as her father.

Albert was embarrassed. He glanced around the bar to see if there were looks of amusement on other people's faces. There weren't. Her father was obviously a familiar sight. James Rhodes was about fifty. Both in age and waistline. In his own words, he was seven and a half gin bottles tall—"Gordon's, of course."

Rhodes was wearing his drinking clothes. The shaggy mohair sports jacket needed a shave almost as much as Rhodes himself. Its bright check clashed garishly with a flowered shirt worn outside a pair of striped morning-suit trousers. On his sockless feet were a pair of hand-made sandals. But it was the other end of Victoria's father which increased Albert's confusion. He was grey, where he had hair—which was only on the sides and round the back of his head. Where he didn't have hair of his own, he wore a wig. This would have looked less eccentric had the toupee not been made twenty years before to match his surviving hair—when it was red. Now it sat on his scalp like a ruffled hen on a grey nest.

Rhodes pulled out a small handful of money and searched. "Got any sixpences?" he asked.

Albert handed him a couple. Rhodes wandered over to the fruit machine.

"Daddy's a shocker," said Victoria. "He's never really grown responsible. He got slung out of the Navy's Legal Department because they said he drank more rum than the whole of the dockyard. He made the fleet contractor rich. Then my mother ran off with the contractor. Daddy's never touched rum since."

Rhodes had then set up business as a solicitor in London. In order to avoid excessive income tax, he'd insisted his clients paid him a portion of their bills in gin. Unfortunately, his local tradesmen were unwilling to accept settlement of his debts in the same good spirit.

Eventually, he was spending so much time fighting his own legal battles that he was unable to accept work from his regular clients. And when Victoria left her boarding school, he decided to retire to the Scillies. Now his Naval pension, and the occasional legal work he did for the Islands' market gardeners enabled him to live comfortably.

Rhodes never held a gin glass stationary. It was either going up, or going down. At the moment it was going down—empty. But Albert noticed another in reserve, ready, on the bar.

"Have a gin," said Rhodes. "Make it two, large ones,"

16

he told the barman. "Don't want another beer yet, do you?" he asked Victoria.

Albert didn't have time to tell him that he'd rather have a beer himself.

"Don't want any watery muck in it?" Rhodes asked, as he passed Albert the glass. Albert decided to say nothing, and, as he didn't like gin anyway, downed it in one swig to Rhodes's "cheers!"

"My round," said Albert quickly, before Rhodes had time to re-order.

Looking at Albert through the bottom of his glass, the solicitor shrewdly weighed him up. Victoria's few young men had been thin, pale and schoolboyish. This one was different. He had a self-assurance that worried Rhodes. And a Cockney charm.

Victoria was an attractive girl, with few things to occupy her. As a child, their holidays on the islands had caused him enough worry—diving and swimming off dangerous rocks, sailing in rough seas in small boats. Now the worries would grow, rather than decrease. He would have to contend with annual romances with odd young men. He hoped that the things she'd learnt at school had prepared her for this sort of encounter.

Neither Albert, nor his Island, particularly interested Rhodes. The Island was useless, as was probably this young man. Foul Rock was nothing more than a shipping hazard, Albert probably even more of a threat to his daughter. Rhodes felt, however, that by meeting him, he might, by brief show of personality, instil just sufficient fear to guarantee her protection. The fact that Albert owned Victoria's favourite Island gave him an edge which Rhodes didn't enjoy.

However, he was pleasant to him, and Albert, investing in his future with Victoria, allowed Rhodes to beat him twice at darts.

The following morning Victoria and Albert met early for another trip to the Island. This time the girl acted as guide. She pointed out the pools that trapped fish, where small crabs could be found under rocks, and the sun traps where the water was hot.

Victoria was good with her speargun. They swam

through the labyrinth of kelp, hunting silver bass that played in the surf. They raked into deep gulleys in the hope of finding lobsters, and they lay in the sun for hours, talking about anything.

For the next few days, they visited the Island together. Every evening was spent in the pub. Rhodes, realising that he held a losing brief, gracefully returned to the comfort of the saloon bar.

Saturday, June 15th, was an historic day. Albert felt that it was going to be, even before he got out of bed. He lay, looking at the cracked ceiling of his room, his hands behind his head, and contemplated. Victoria wanted him. This was made clear the day before. Albert decided to play it cool. Today, he hoped, was going to be very special. He swung out of bed and stretched. He could hear the seagulls marshalling themselves on the roof of a nearby barn. The sun was already warm. It was only six o'clock.

He washed, then shaved carefully. A quick squirt of deodorant, the slightest touch of talcum and he was almost ready. He chose a striped blue and white T-shirt and a clean pair of jeans. He hurried to the harbour and sat on the low wall to wait.

Victoria stood naked in front of the long mirror of her rosewood wardrobe. Albert wanted her. It was made clear the day before. He didn't know it, but he was going to get her today. She turned sideways and put her hands on her breasts. How would it feel when a man did this? she wondered. The girls had talked about sex, after lights out, in their dormitory. They'd all read the Kama Sutra—and sniggered. They'd tried the positions on the dormitory floor, and thought they were impossible. Which permutation would he choose? she asked herself.

Would it be romantic? Would he undress her, or would she have to do it? Would he tell her he loved her? Yes, he would, she decided. She'd make him. She thought she would please him. She was going to try.

No underclothes. She chose her smallest bikini and topped it with the pale cotton dress that boosted her tan. She opened the bottle of Blue Grass perfume that Aunt

18

Dorothy had given her for Christmas. She almost showered with it. She smiled at the thought. If only Aunt Dorothy knew what it was being used for.

She wriggled her toes into her sandals. Grabbed her packed beach bag and hurried out.

She arrived only a few minutes after him. She was slightly flushed and a little out of breath and he suspected that she had run down from her father's cottage on the hillside.

Albert checked the petrol in the outboard and the spare can, wiped the dew from the leatherette seats and then warmed up the motor. The boat was fast. It would do almost forty miles an hour.

He drove it fiercely towards the Island, feeling the thud of the speed-hardened waves under the hull. Victoria sat close. The nearness of her body warmed him where he had been chilled by the sharp morning air. They were both excited.

The sun was still fairly low by the time they arrived. But it was warmer now that they'd lost the breeze caused by the speed of the boat. They clambered onto the shingle floor of the gulley and dragged the bow a little way up onto the rocks. They tied it to a small, sharp pinnacle, and scrambled onto the central pleateau of the Island. Victoria took Albert's hand.

They reached the place where Albert had first stood to survey his kingdom. He stopped and pulled Victoria towards him.

"Sit here for a while."

Victoria slipped off her cotton dress.

"Oil me," she said.

Albert fumbled through the bag to find the bottle. He massaged the oil onto Victoria's shoulders and arms.

He handed her the container. She passed it back.

"What about the rest of me?" she pouted.

"This little pig," said Albert, starting with her toes. He stopped at her knees.

"Go on," said Victoria.

"No," said Albert.

"Give me your hand."

19

Albert held it out. She took his wrist and turned it over until she could pour more oil into his palm.

"I don't want to touch it. I want to comb my hair in a minute," she said.

She guided his oil-filled hand into position, and smoothed it over her thighs.

"See, that didn't hurt at all, did it?"

Albert gulped, and hoped he didn't have to stand up.

He lit his first cigarette of the day and looked at Victoria, now lying next to him, face downwards on the smooth rock. Her face was hidden by her hair which she had combed loose. He knew that she was watching him through the golden haze.

He reached out his arm until it rested heavily on her oiled back. He unclipped her bra, and then slid the straps apart. They stuck, for a moment, oily, to her brown skin, then dropped to the rock. The rounded side of her breast was only slightly paler than her shoulder.

Albert pushed himself around until he was sitting close against her. He jabbed his cigarette at the rock, then he leant down until he could kiss the nape of her neck. She rolled over, leaving her bikini top beneath her.

He could feel the small hardness of her nipples against his chest. Her hands drew him towards her, then slipped downwards behind him, beneath his jeans. The hands moved around his hips, making him wince as they crossed the nerves of his stomach. The girl pushed herself up against him, forcing him backwards until she lay on top of him. She pulled her lips away from his, and kissed his throat, chest and shoulders, just like it said in the Kama Sutra.

Her hands found the zip of his jeans and then smoothed them away over his thighs. Her lips searched lower and lower. Albert reached down and pressed her head against him. Her soft hair fell on either side of his hips. He coiled it with his hands and pulled her face up to his own. Now they were both naked. Victoria had slipped out of her own briefs. She fell back. Now they were separated only by the slippery coating of suntan oil. She jerked.

"Ouch."

Albert jumped. She'd shouted in his ear.

20

"Something's bitten me." She sat up and twisted to look over her shoulder. "You didn't put your cigarette out."

"I'm sorry," he mumbled inadequately, his interest diminishing.

"It hurts."

He dabbed carefully at her back.

"You've got a blister," he said. "Can I put something on it?"

"It stings. Maybe if we go for a swim it'll stop."

"Now?" asked Albert.

"We'll come up here later."

"Women!" said Albert.

They carried their clothes down to the boat and left them on the seats. When they came out of the water they didn't dress. There wasn't really much point. They were alone, and they both knew that they would make love soon.

Around mid-day Albert noticed that he was feeling chilly. For the past two and a half hours he hadn't looked further than the few inches that separated him from Victoria. They still hadn't made love, but were lying snuggled together. He now raised his head and looked out over the rocks.

The sea disappeared into a low mist that hung over the water. Visibility was only about fifty yards. The face of the sea was flat, and it was strangely quiet. Cedric, the herring-gull, was sitting on his usual boulder.

"Fog," said Albert. "Maybe we'll both be marooned this time."

Victoria sat up and shivered. "It won't last very long," she told him. "We often get these summer sea mists around here. It'll probably blow clear in an hour or so. Cuddle me, first...."

2 Captain Vorolokov pushed a hairy hand under his thick sweater, and scratched an even hairier stomach with his blunt fingers. He was day dreaming. He had been a fisherman for a long time. A real fisherman. He could remember when Russian trawlers only went out to catch fish. He'd enjoyed those days. Days when he'd hand-hauled in a net, packed with shivering cod, to be loaded into the holds and taken back to the markets of the White Sea ports. At last, he was on his way back to the North Sea and the English Channel, waters which he remembered from his service in the wartime Archangel convoys.

Now he was as much a military seaman as the man who captained a warship. In fact, Vorolokov was an extremely successful military seaman. He had risen from the fo'castle of a fishing boat, to captain of the latest "trawler" in the Soviet Navy.

The *Dmitri Kirov* was a trawler only in hull design. She carried no fishing gear. Her gunwhales hid machine-gun mountings. Her stern cabin housed a depthcharge launcher. Her for'ard hatch contained a battery of heat-seeking surface-to-air missiles. The entire centre section of the boat concealed a cradle capable of directing a thirty foot rocket to a target twenty miles away.

But her impressive armoury was little more than a ribcage protecting the real heart of the ship—a collection of the most sophisticated interception equipment and listening devices Soviet scientists had ever produced. So sensitive that they could follow the subtle movements of ships far beyond the horizon. So technically advanced that the scientists feared the full potential would be limited by human inadequacies. So expensive, the trawler rivalled, in cost and technological skill, a major Soviet space probe.

The *Dmitri Kirov* was off to join the Nato Fleet exercises in the Atlantic. She hadn't been invited. Her job was to shadow the war fleet's activities. She would identify ships. Note armaments. Count air-strength of carriers. Intercept and record messages. Pin-point radar and radio stations. Check underwater movements with her hydrophones. And relay all the information back to Moscow. The Nato ships already knew she was coming.

In Leningrad the week before, Vorolokov had kissed his sister goodbye, shaken hands with his brother-in-law, and put out to sea. When he opened the usual orders, he was surprised to find a letter from the Fleet Commander accompanying them. Its final paragraph had made him screw the letter into a ball and throw it angrily into the corner of the cabin: "There is no need to ask you to obey, without question, the orders of Professor Ushakov and his three Comrade Scientists."

At dusk, the *Dmitri Kirov* sailed.

Saturday, June 15th: A short, stubble-chinned man nudged Vorolokov rather too hard in the ribs, and pushed a stained mug of coffee into his hand. It was Boris the cook.

Boris was ugly. His friends felt they were being kind to him when they described him as such. The jackboot which had broken his nose had actually improved his face, and stitches high on his cheek gave his left profile a permanent smile.

Vorolokov and he waged a continuous good-natured war. They had sailed together for many years.

Boris pretended he hated the sea even more than he hated his captain. It was either this job, he argued, or sweeping the streets of his home town—cooks were two-a-kopek on dry land, and there were few restaurants to employ them.

In any case, he claimed, strictly speaking he wasn't a cook. Like Vorolokov he'd started sea-life as a deckhand on a fishing boat. Their cook was dangerously bad. On his last voyage, after a third of the crew had gone down with food poisoning, the cook conveniently fell overboard. Boris inherited his job.

The war between him and Vorolokov had begun on the day when the captain found seagull feathers in a bowl of borsch. Boris claimed that they had blown into the cooking pot. Vorolokov didn't believe him.

The crew were a bizarre assortment. Most were related. Mischa, the trawler's bos'n, was also the senior family member. He was uncle to Vasili, and uncle by marriage to Sacha, who was the first mate. Sacha was married to Mischa's niece. Mischa was also a cousin of his bos'n's mate, Lev. Josef, one of the leading hands, claimed family relationships to them all by an aunt's marriage to Mischa's brother. Boris was Josef's uncle. The remaining crew members were more distantly related. Vorolokov was a foreigner, born in a different town, and the other cuckoo was young Igor—a Cossack by his own adoption, if not by birth. He was an orphan.

Between them they possessed a mostly useless collection of talents. Lev loved dogs. Rasputin, his mute alsatian, went with him on all his trips. Lev did his barking and growling for him. Mischa claimed to know a secret Mongolian way of breaking a man's neck with a casual twist. He'd never, in fact, put this into practice. Boris, who didn't know the secret, had escaped from a concentration camp in Poland and was known to have broken several guards' necks. Vasili could dislocate his shoulder at will—and did so whenever he needed time off. Igor was a natural dancer.

They all claimed to be able to smell shoals of fish, ice floes and mudbanks, and identify the countries they sailed past by the different odours that drifted to them over the sea.

They all worked well. Vorolokov had little or no trouble. On shore, they drank together. At sea, they knew and understood each other.

There were some on board the *Dmitri Kirov*, however, whom the trawlermen did not understand. They were the four scientists who operated the complex armoury of the ship and the even more complicated listening instruments.

Vorolokov met them only occasionally. The scientists ate together in their own mess, while he took his main meals with the other members of his crew, or while standing at his post on the bridge

The scientists were strange. They talked in a language only they could comprehend. And they made Vorolokov feel ignorant in their company. He completely mistrusted their below-decks navigation.

Being, basically, a fisherman, Vorolokov was able to plot his course from one fishing ground to another. He was never lost. And, although his course-laying tended to be, by scientific standards, perhaps unorthodox, he always found his way. He'd caught good, sometimes record, catches of fish, and always got the boat and her crew safely home.

He worked instinctively with a combination of the sun, the stars, the seasons, the currents, occasionally his compass, and, more rarely, with his charts.

Now on this, his most important command, he was not allowed to choose his own course. The intercom would buzz, and a strange voice would order him to change direction a few degrees this way, or that. Resentfully, he would comply, or pass on the orders to the steersman.

For the past week, ever since they had left Leningrad, he had known only where they'd been. His course was a series of zigzag lines on the scientists' charts.

Vorolokov was annoyed and frustrated as they sailed through and away from his fishing grounds.

He knew nothing of the weapons on board his ship. He knew they were there, and he knew they were effective and important. They weren't under his control. He couldn't even open a hatch without permission. All the weapons and instruments were controlled by the Whiteshirts, the crew's name for the scientists. Vorolokov knew he was a puppet.

He spat a mouthful of coffee grounds over the rail. And determined to do something about the cook before his next voyage.

Below decks, in the small square of a radio cabin, Tanya Suvorova drew another face on the nail of her left thumb, then leant back and pushed the earphones away from her face. It seemed to the twenty-two-year-old that she was spending her whole life in the three metres square radio room. A fluorescent tube in the deck-head was the sole means of lighting.

She rarely saw daylight except when she went above for fresh air at the end of her watch. For the rest of the time, she sat at the radio table, wearing a headset.

At the moment she felt a little guilty. She'd spent the last fifteen minutes listening, with pleasure, to Western music on one of the civil broadcasting wavelengths.

Tanya was Vorolokov's pet, the daughter he never had. She was ebony-haired, with grey eyes that reminded him of the misty lakes of his childhood home on the edges of the White Sea. Her voice was soft, so soft he always had to hold his head close to the speaking tube when she spoke.

A buzzer, on the board in front of her, gave out a sharp chirrup of a signal. Tanya stubbed her cigarette and took up the earphones. Over the static she recognised coded greetings from the depot ship *Ayat*. They were due to rendezvous later in the day.

She acknowledged and signed off briefly. Then flicked up the intercom key and reported to Ushakov the position given by the *Ayat*.

Ushakov walked over to the indicator screen and located the mother ship some twenty-one miles off their port bow. He plotted the new course. Then he called Vorolokov on the bridge, gave him his instructions. "We will be alongside in an hour and a half."

Vorolokov threw up his arms, and muttered something blasphemous. The steersman swung the wheel a few degrees, and Vorolokov checked the new bearing on a compass. They'd now passed through the English Channel. As usual, he wondered whether the whiteshirts below knew what they were doing.

Sixty-seven minutes later, the *Dmitri Kirov* ran into a fog-bank. Vorolokov signalled to the radar room, and told Ushakov. He received an almost immediate reply that the depot ship *Ayat* was directly ahead in an otherwise clear sea. . . .

Boris left the galley with another trayful of oily-looking coffee. He took a cheroot stub from his mouth, and dogged the ashy end into the largest mug. He stirred it with his finger, and wiped his hand on his grubby smock. Both sides of his face smiled.

He lurched his way up the steep companionway to the bridge, and barged open the door with his heavy shoulder.

He waved the mug in front of the captain. Vorolokov took it, and grunted a word of thanks. It puzzled him why he always thanked Boris for his appalling coffee. He decided it was more a matter of habit than appreciation.

Vorolokov let the bitter, hot liquid sear its way down his throat. He leant forward against the compass binnacle, balancing himself against the roll of the ship.

Boris watched him.

The half-empty mug clattered to the deck. Coffee formed a lake on the sacred planking. Vorolokov's jaw dropped open. Siberian tin glinted among his teeth. His face turned white. His massive, hairy hands clenched on the polished horns of the compass.

Boris was paralysed with the fear of the awful retribution he was certain would overtake him.

It was not so much a crash as an eruption. There was a discordant peal of tearing, buckling metal and grinding rock. A bulkhead leapt towards Boris. A fire extinguisher sprang from its bracket and burst, fogging everything with powder. Through half-conscious eyes, the cook watched Vorolokov levitate and smash through the chart table and the bridge windows. The steersman's body hurtled against the wheel. He slumped over it unconscious, his sweater caught on a bent spoke.

There were shouts from below as men were bounced about by the impact. Heavy equipment tore from mountings. Furniture and crockery destroyed themselves in a tangle of wreckage. The shackles holding the anchor snapped. It dropped. The chain rattled out. Then there was silence.

Vorolokov opened his eyes. He was suspended halfway through the glass panelling at the front of the wheelhouse. His head was wedged tightly between an upright and the mechanism that operated the huge windscreen wipers. Slowly, he levered himself up and looked along the now convoluted foredeck. Fuel oil fountained from a fractured pipe on the deck just in front of him. It was chaos.

He looked farther ahead. There was no sea. Just a rocky plateau. Two small, surprised and naked figures stood hand-in-hand looking up at him from beyond the trawler's crumpled bow.

The *Dmitri Kirov,* pride of the supreme Soviet Navy's spy fleet, now occupied a large slice of the Island won by Albert's uncle from Fatty Hagan in a poker game.

3

Victoria and Albert, both naked, stared up at the tortured bow of the trawler rearing over them. There was a thick silence, broken only by the dripping of water from the torn hull.

They had been lying on the plateau, their thoughts identical. They had each brought the other to the very point of seduction. Victoria had made Albert work hard. She wasn't in a hurry. She knew her Kama Sutra. She wanted to savour every foreplay, to make it last.

"Is this how it should be? Am I doing it right?" She had been anxious, trembling to Albert's experienced touch.

Albert had finally manoeuvered himself gently into position and begun a mental count-down. Five, four, three. . . . A muffled sound in the mist had made him look up. Slicing through the haze towards them was a ship. Instinctively, Albert leapt off the bewildered Victoria. The approaching bow, aiming at them, sheared into the island. He dragged the panting girl to her feet. Spray from the steel hull showered them as it juddered to rest only a few yards away. The anchor shattered rock at Albert's feet as it catapulted from its chocks. It was buried by the chain that clanked after it.

A bearded face appeared and stared down at them. It was blood-streaked, and drooled a brown, treacly liquid.

"Oi, Chichester!" Albert called up, furiously. "You're trespassing."

The head looked at them in astonishment. It raised two large clenched hands and banged them down on the rail of the ship. Then it disappeared abruptly. It came back almost immediately, this time accompanied by a ruffled female head wearing earphones with a short length of wire dangling from them. Her nose was bleeding and thin trickles of blood ran down both sides of her mouth, giving it a sinister, red Genghis Khan moustache. More heads joined them until the whole bow of the ship resembled the gallery of a music hall.

Albert suddenly realised that he was nude, and clasped himself modestly. Victoria stood, staring in amazement at the dark grey ship.

"Vot, in front of our ship, are you doing?" asked a voice stained with an Old Kent Road accent.

"You're parked on our clothes. If you'll back off a bit we can get dressed. And, I think you've squashed our sandwiches. They were in our boat."

The heads disappeared. It was impossible for Albert to see what was happening on the deck high above. He unclasped himself. Victoria continued to stare in hypnotised disbelief. He gripped her shoulders and jolted her out of her stupor.

"I think I left my sunglasses down there," was all she could say, looked at the gulley now filled entirely by the trawler.

"At a time like this," mumbled Albert. He took her arm and led her down towards the scrambled remains of her boat. A twisted steering wheel stuck out from under the keel of the ship. Shattered whiskers of glass-fibre were strewn down the cleft of the rock. The outboard engine had been rolled into a horse-shoe.

The only sign of their clothing was a blue and white sleeve from Albert's T-shirt. Victoria's sunglasses were lying undamaged, in the wreckage. She examined them carefully, then smiled vacantly at Albert as she put them on.

He pulled the starting cord off the outboard engine and tied it around his waist. Then he tucked the blue and white sleeve in, front and rear, like a loin cloth. There was nothing more they could salvage.

He walked to the stern of the trawler. It was completely out of the water. Only the tip of a folded propeller blade touched the sea. One side of the hull was split along twenty feet of its length where a wedge of rock had cut through the metal plates like a laser beam. He walked back towards the plateau and looked up, for the first time, at the name on the bow.

"Screw me. It's a bloody Russian!"

A rope ladder unrolled over the side of the ship and slapped against the rocks. A sea-boot appeared, followed by a heavy body and the hairy face of Vorolokov. A small procession followed him down.

With a great deal of muttering, the damage to the trawler's hull was examined. Albert didn't need to know Russian to realise that juicy oaths and blame were being directed, for the most part, at a white-shirted young man.

For a while it looked as though the young man and the big seaman might translate their argument to blows. The woman, still wearing her earphones and her sanguine Mongolian moustache, walked between them and, pointing at Albert, said something to them both. Albert suddenly wished he was holidaying, as usual, in Clacton.

"Goot arftermoon," she said. "How did you managing move the Island in front of us so quickly?"

Albert was shaken by this piece of female logic.

The cutting blast of a ship's siren from behind him made the whole party jump. Albert twisted round. His stomach taughtened in panic. He half expected to see a ship heading into the Island from the other direction. He was already finding Foul Rock a little too crowded.

Through the lifting mist, and only four hundred yards away, anchored bow and stern, in line with the course of the trawler, was a huge tanker. At her masthead flew the red flag of the USSR.

As they watched, a launch was lowered and motored towards the Island. The stranded Russian crew moved down to meet it. Their conversation with the men on board began while they were still fifty yards away.

The visitors made a rapid survey of the trawler's damage. It was plain that at least Victoria's presence had been noted by the new arrivals. There were several distinctly lecherous looks in her direction. But she felt anonymous behind her sunglasses. Albert had the uncomfortable feeling that the Russians would have been a lot happier had he and Victoria been squashed, along with their small motor-boat.

Eventually, the party made their way over to him.

"What are you doing here?" asked the uniformed officer in almost accent-less English.

"You're on my Island. You've smashed our boat and ruined all our gear. My bird's got no drawers."

The officer gave a curt order to a tall Russian at his side. The deck-hand stripped off his huge, oily sweater and handed it to Victoria. She turned and pulled it on. It fitted her like a huge, seaman's oily sweater, but the effect was erotic—no one could forget she still had no drawers.

The party made its way to the side of the trawler, and began to climb aboard. Albert and Victoria, uncertain what to do, waited at the foot of the ladder.

A moment later, the female head poked itself over the gunwale and invited them up. Albert led the way.

"Come, please."

The female, and a stocky man with a bent nose and a smile on one side of his face, escorted them into a cabin.

"You must have share this," she waved at a two-tier berth. "I hope you not minding having up bunk."

"Such consideration," said Albert, eyeing Victoria.

"Sit, please. Vodka, yes?"

Albert nodded to her. "On the rocks."

"Where, please?"

Albert smiled, and sat down, realising suddenly that he was uncomfortably sunburnt in an unusual place.

A couple of greasy glasses were thrust into their hands by Bent Nose. A bottle was placed on the table. Albert took a sip at the clear liquid the girl poured for him.

"Niet. Like this." She downed her drink in one swig. Albert and Victoria copied her.

Twenty minutes later the bottle was half empty.

Albert guessed that the female was trying to soften them up. But he didn't care. He felt distinctly happier, though it flashed through his mind that they gave condemned men a drink of spirits before execution. He wondered whether the vodka would anaesthetise his throbbing backside.

The cabin door was pushed open. They were joined by the owner of the beard and the uniformed officer from the tanker.

"This," said the female, pointing to the beard, "is Trawler Captain Vorolokov. And this is Fleet Captain-Commander Nevskii. I am Tanya Suvorova, radio operator."

Albert introduced himself and Victoria.

31

Vorolokov explained that, despite the apparently severe damage, they hoped to refloat the trawler the next day. They intended to work through the night, welding fresh plates over the slit in the hull. She would then be towed back to Leningrad for repairs.

Victoria thought the Russian captain was warm and friendly. He spoke good English.

"Our accident was radar error," he said. "Most inconveniencing to everybody. We much regret destruction of your boat. Our Embassy in London will arrange compensation. Tomorrow we take you to your homeland. Meantime, please be our guests."

Albert thanked them for their courtesy.

The three Russians left the cabin.

Tanya returned shortly afterwards with an armful of clothes. "For you," she said. She left.

Albert removed his loincloth, and looked ruefully, over his shoulder at the reflection of his glowing behind in the locker mirror.

As Monarch of Foul Rock, he thought, he'd order his physicians to post a bulletin on the palace railings. It would say King Albert was indisposed following a riding mishap. How could he admit to his adoring subjects that he'd burnt his arse attempting to screw a bird al fresco?

They dressed. Albert found the rough cloth of the dungarees chafed the backs of his legs.

Sounds of activity made him look out of one of the portholes. He saw a crowd of seamen dragging welding equipment towards the boat. Above, he could hear more men at work.

The noises grew louder, as torn and damaged sections of the hull were cut away with oxy-acetylene torches. Metal banged as the engineers shuffled new plates into position. The noise, reverberating through the cabin, drove Albert and Victoria outside.

The sun was setting. But arc-lights on the rocks and on deck painted the area with light. Albert thought that, had it not been for the noise, it would have been romantic. Instead, it was grotesque.

Orange tracers of metal sprayed from the hull, showering

the sweating welders, and dying dull-red on the rocks at their feet.

The plates shimmered and blushed as the blue-white jets of the torches cut away scarred metal.

Red fire reflected from dark goggles. Pale cones of smoke moved like wraiths with the soft breeze.

Macabre shadows heaved and flung themselves among the rocks like some nightmarish ballet as their owners went about their work. The Island quivered with activity. It was like peering into the devil's smithy.

Albert leaned against the gunwale, and unconsciously slipped his arm around Victoria's waist as he watched, fascinated. The sun sank unnoticed.

Tanya appeared at their side, and beckoned them down to the Mess. Vorolokov was already there. He made Victoria sit on his left. Tanya took her usual seat on his right. Albert gingerly lowered himself next to her. He felt at home, wearing his borrowed seaman's clothing.

Georgian wine came with the Russian pancakes and salted herrings. Vorolokov commanded the conversation He spoke affectionately of his visits to Britain during the war. That was how he learned to speak English, he explained.

"In those days, there no English taught in Russian schools," he said. "Now, everything different."

For the first time since the shock of the trawler's arrival, Victoria began to relax. She liked Vorolokov. He was the first Russian she'd ever met. She was now enjoying the adventure, but she knew her father would be worrying because she hadn't returned.

After coffee and more vodka, Vorolokov excused himself to get back to supervising the repairs to the hull. Tanya, it seemed, would be working late in the radio room. Victoria and Albert returned to their cabin.

The noise was now like an iron foundry.

Albert wondered how Douglas Fairbanks—Senior, of course—would deal with the situation. . . . He'd slide quietly out of the sea at the far end of the Island, sabre in one hand, a lighted bomb in the other. He would silence the guard with a quick, almost nochalant, blow. Albert Fairbanks would toss the bomb and when it exploded under the ship's magazine, he would charge among the bewildered crew with his sword. In seconds there would be no ship, no sounds of life to disturb him on his Island. He would win the war. And get the girl.

Albert was startled out of his day dream.

"It's too noisy to sleep. D'you think they'll lend us a Monopoly set?"

Albert looked down at her as she sat on the low bunk beside him. She was smiling. She reached up and pulled him down by his belt. Albert kissed her. "I don't fancy Monopoly," he said. He was about to suggest a better method of night-passing, when the door opened. It was Tanya again. 'You don't mind, I off duty now. I sleep." She dropped, fully dressed, into the single bunk on the far side of the cabin.

Albert groaned, and climbed into the top bunk, above Victoria. He lay on his stomach, his burnt back was too painful. He was in the right position again. Victoria was underneath him. He cursed the three foot gap and the mattress between them.

Victoria was awakened by someone gently shaking her. Tanya stood there. She was carrying coffee.

"Please be ready soon. We take off the boat shortly."

It was just after five o'clock. The day was still thin and hungry. Outside, the activity continued. Albert and Victoria walked onto the deck. All round the Island were ships— Russian ships. At least a dozen were anchored around the eastern end.

A tired Vorolokov waved to them from below. They climbed down to him. He was standing, looking at the new metal sheets on the hull.

"An untidy job," he apologised. "But it will get us home. In a few minutes they start tow us off. Please stand at other end of Island, so you not get hurt."

Thick ropes and wire hawsers stretched from the beached *Dmitri Kirov* into the water in the direction of the anchored ships. The trawler seemed to be part of a gigantic web. A siren gave a shriek. Anchor chains chattered. The ships, joined to the stern of the imprisoned vessel, manoeuvred until they radiated away from her. Two short siren notes gave the signal for the tow to begin.

34

Albert and Victoria backed away from the hull.

White water churned behind the heaving vessels. The hawsers stiffened into bars of brown steel.

Albert could see Vorolokov on deck, gesticulating, and shouting orders.

For tedious seconds, nothing happened. Then, there was a series of sharp bangs as some of the tow lines parted. The bow of the damaged trawler shuddered and tilted. There were more explosions. Great lengths of rope hurtled, whip-lashing back over the *Dmitri Kirov,* smashing away deck fittings. There was a final gunshot as the last hawser broke.

White dust of powdered rock swirled around the still captive trawler.

Two hours later, the towing vessels were in position to try again. This time, however, they were joined by their depot ship, the tanker.

As before, the siren heralded the action. The ships strained. Again there was a shuddering, then a noise like a small cannon being fired. A tow line thrashed back across the deck, tearing off a bollard and hurling it through the corner of the bridge. The explosion was followed by another. This time the entire after-deckhouse was carried away, re-vealing the ominous barrel of the depthcharge launcher.

Then Albert heard the trawler scream. Unearthly and terrifying, it echoed round the Island. The bow lifted eight feet clear of the ground, hung for a moment, then crashed down with a thunderous splintering of rock and metal. A compressed air whistle on the trawler's bridge added to the noise. The towing boats cut their engines. The trawler lay dead, still in the grip of the Island. Her back was broken. The final towing attempt had literally pulled her apart.

Back on the wrecked ship, Albert was told: "She is here for good. We have decided to unload the equipment."

"You can't leave this great heap of old iron on my Island," said Albert. "This is fly tipping and it's illegal in this country."

"We have no choice," Vorolokov told him sadly. "But once we unloaded, maybe we can blow hull to pieces for you before we leave."

A shout from the rocks stopped the conversation.

"It's Daddy," said Victoria.

She ran to the side of the ship. Rhodes was standing at the foot of the rope ladder. Beside him stood the oil-skin clad coxswain of the local lifeboat.

Rhodes was a mixture of anger and relief. When the couple had failed to return, he had notified the coastguards. Before dawn, he had joined the lifeboat crew in a search.

"I'll horsewhip the young dog," he told the coxswain.

They landed near the stricken trawler, and he was horrified to see the remains of his powerboat scattered in the gully, mingled with shreds of clothing, and Albert's crushed binoculars.

Victoria slid down the ladder and hugged him. Albert followed. He explained what had happened.

Rhodes sat on a rock and listened. His shrewd eyes scrutinised the strange aerials, domes and complicated antennae on the trawler's superstructure.

At last he stood up. He groped in his pocket and fished out a gin-filled hip flask—the largest Albert had ever seen. It looked like a Foreign Legionnaire's water bottle. He unscrewed the drinking cup and handed it empty to Albert. Then he swigged deeply from the bottle before passing it over.

"I think I can make you rich, my boy." He prodded Albert in the chest to emphasise each word. "You need my experienced guidance. They can't remove a barnacle from that hulk without a specific ruling from the Receiver of Wrecks—and that's you, on this bit of rock."

He put both his hands on the top of his head and pushed his wig forward in the best courtroom manner.

"As I read it, this Island is subject only to your laws. Leave this to me."

He turned away, then looked back at Albert. "As your country's Attorney-General, of course. . . ."

Rhodes walked over to Vorolokov and Ushakov, who were briefing the crew on unloading the trawler.

"I want to speak to the officer in charge," he said firmly.

"I am the captain."

Rhodes assumed the officious mannerisms of his profession.

"Good. I have to inform you that you cannot unload a single piece of equipment until compensation has been assessed by the International Courts. I am the legal advisor to the owner of this Island, and I need not point out the implications if you fail to observe this warning."

A cunning look came into Vorolokov's eyes.

"Salvage?" he asked.

"Salvage. And compensation," corrected Rhodes.

"Can he do this to us?" asked the scientist in Russian.

"Yes, but I hoped we'd get away with it."

Ushakov shrugged his shoulders. The two men climbed wearily aboard the unhappy trawler.

Tanya put her head round the door of her radio cabin and watched the dejected Vorolokov approach.

"Captain-Commander Nevskii wants to know when to expect the first boatload of equipment."

"Tell him we can't unload anything. We've got a mad lawyer here threatening to nail a writ on the ship. I was afraid this might happen when I saw the lifeboat arrive. Nevskii will have to sort it out."

Tanya relayed the message.

"He wants to talk to you," she said.

Vorolokov winced, and picked up the radio-telephone.

Rhodes, Albert and Victoria sat on the rocks close to the gleaming lifeboat.

Tanya called down from the deck of the trawler.

"Captain-Commander Nevskii ask you go over his ship and talk."

"Sorry," Rhodes called back. "We are not prepared to leave our territory to discuss this. He must come here."

He turned to Albert. "No matter what happens, we've got to stay put. That's right, isn't it, Bill?"

The final remark was made to the lifeboatman who had come ashore with him.

"Aye, we knows about salvage, m'dear," nodded Bill.

The discussion, when Nevskii finally appeared, was deviously legal. The Russian insisted that he had every right to remove his country's property from the Island. Rhodes was equally firm that it should remain. Victoria was thrilled to see that her father's argument was not affected by the armed guards who had accompanied the officer.

At length, the solicitor walked across to Albert.

"Are you prepared to sell or lease part of the Island?"

"What's it worth?"

"Don't worry. You can leave it to me. I'll make the best deal I can."

He turned back to the Russian.

"The owner of this country is prepared to lease you the damaged half, containing your trawler, for six million roubles.'

The Russian looked stunned—as stunned as Albert, who, although he didn't know how much it was, thought it sounded a lot.

"It's over a million pounds," Victoria whispered, remembering her recent A-level exams.

The Russian stared hard at Rhodes.

"I will contact my Government immediately."

4 Rhodes watched Nevskii's stiff back as the Russian attempted to march arrogantly over the rough ground to his boat, followed by his armed guard. He was obviously very angry. He splashed into the shallows and boarded the cutter in one movement. One of the men pushed the boat clear with an oar, and they steered towards the *Ayat*. Nevskii stared ahead, refusing even a backward glance at the Island.

Rhodes shed his legal mannerisms. "We're going to win, we're going to win." He jigged up and down. Albert could see daylight between the scalp and red wig.

"We've only got to negotiate now. The Russians know they'll have to pay in the end. They'll want to sort it out before the West starts taking an interest." He poured himself a celebratory drink from his hip flask, and went on: "This isn't a fishing boat. It's a spy ship. It's probably got millions of pounds' worth of equipment on board. The Russians know the Yanks would love to get their hands on it, so they'll want it dismantled and away as quickly as possible."

He looked at his watch. "I'll go back to St Mary's with the lifeboat," he said. "You two stay put. And don't go on the trawler again. Sorry, you'll have to go hungry till I get back. I'll get food and a tent, and we'll stick it out here for as long as it takes. I'll be back this evening. Oh! And we must have your deeds. Where are they?"

Albert told him they were in his suitcase at his digs. "Stick some clothes in, I'll need them, anyway," he said.

Rhodes boarded the lifeboat.

Albert called after him. "Better tell Mrs Pengelly I won't be home for supper tonight, either."

He wondered whether his landlady would still charge him for his two missed evening meals. He suddenly felt guilty for thinking this; after all, he was only a few hours away from being a millionaire. At the same time, he thought of the small pokerwork plaque that hung over the fireplace at home which read—"Money is the root of all evil."

Albert walked Victoria to the western end of the Island. From here the trawler was hidden by the rise of the plateau. They swam and sunbathed again. Now they really did have a lot to talk about.

"What are you going to do with all the money?" she asked.

Albert looked blank.

"I mean, you could buy almost anything."

Now he looked worried.

"I had a friend once," he told her. "He won £150 on the football pools. It ruined him."

She laughed.

"Seriously," he said. "He went right off his rocker. He went abroad for his holiday—it bankrupted him. And it spoiled him for Clacton."

She pressed a slim finger against her forehead and thought.

"You could own two-hundred Rolls Royces. You could spend over £4,000 a day for a year. What do you earn?"

"Oh, after I've paid tax, and things, I end up with about twelve quid a week."

"You could spend ten pounds a day for almost six-hundred years."

"It's not the money that worries me," Albert told her. "It's just that I've never thought I'd ever have much. I don't smoke a lot, and I don't drink much, and I go to the cinema every night of the week. I play soccer and I go dancing when I can. I've got Uncle Alf's house and furniture. I dress all right and I save a bit. God knows what Manny will say when I get back."

"I think I'll have to teach you what to want." She leaned over and bit him gently on the neck.

"I know what I want," he said, grinning at her. "But it looks as though the Russian Navy won't let me have it."

Captain-Commander Nevskii was normally faultlessly dressed. Tall, with grey close-cropped hair, he was a handsome example of the best products of the Soviet Naval Academy. His service record was exceptional. His study of languages was grooming him, he hoped, for the post of naval attaché in one of the Western countries. Canada, for preference—he liked ice-hockey.

His cabin door was locked. He sat at his desk, tie wrenched loose, collar unbuttoned. His jacket sagged over his hunched shoulders. He rested his forehead on the thumb of his left hand, which held a cigarette with a long curve of ash. He stared down at a chart. The small dot, surrounded by a ring of contours that was Foul Rock, stared back.

The ash fell. Angrily he stubbed out the butt and swept the chart and its cargo of ash onto his carpet. He reached into a drawer and pulled out a vacuum flask. Unscrewing the cap, he filled it, almost to its thread, with near frozen vodka. He flushed it down his throat, and lit another cigarette.

His career teetered. Now he waited only for the cable that would relegate him to some dark corner of a Naval Office in a small port. This was the penalty, he knew, for losing even an unimportant ship of his fleet. He couldn't imagine the punishment for losing the vital *Dmitri Kirov*.

The thought of the reaction to his coded signal to the Supreme Naval Command, at home, made him sweat. He topped-up the flask cap and drank again.

He thought of the long years since college. Years when he had often sacrificed his personal feelings to advance his position. He had never married. His parents were dead. He was an only child. His friends were other successful officers. He wondered whether he might have to face the future completely alone.

A sharp knock on the cabin door jarred him from his thoughts.

"Signal officer, sir."

Captain-Commander Nevskii kicked the chart out of sight behind the desk. He tucked the vodka flask away. By the time he had opened the door, his tie was snug against its collar, and he was once more the elegant fleet commander.

41

A hardness came into his eyes as he saw the smiling face of the signal officer.

He snatched the cable and ordered the seaman to wait outside.

"Young bastards," he thought. "It doesn't take long for maggots to pick on a carcass."

He unfolded the signal and read it.

His shoulders twitched. His mouth spread.

He did something completely alien to his austere shipboard life. He exploded into laughter. It rang round the cabin. He clutched at his day bed and sagged onto the mattress. Tears raced down his cheeks. He rolled onto his back and, hugging his knees, tried to focus tear-blurred eyes on the message.

He read again the personal congratulations from the President of the Soviet Praesidium. They were profuse, almost poetic. They were unique. Captain Nevskii had never heard such praise.

Nevskii stood up, a hero and a Rear-Admiral. He had been promoted for doing the impossible. He had acquired, for Russia, a base of vital strategic importance at the foot of Britain, and guarding the entrance to the Atlantic Ocean, the English Channel, the Irish Sea and the Bay of Biscay. Foul Rock was worth a Czar's treasure.

Albert and Victoria stood on the north side of the Island, helping Rhodes unload his supplies. His return from the mainland was like a carnival, and the Russian fishermen standing on the trawler watched.

He arrived in a ski-boat loaded almost to danger point. With him was his chief clerk, Collins, dressed impeccably in black jacket and striped trousers and a pearl-grey tie that caught the sunlight. The solicitor himself looked as though he was off for a day's shark-fishing. He wore white waders, a stunning yellow oilskin and a blue and red cycling cap with the word CINZANO on the front.

Ignoring their Russian audience, he and Collins solemnly searched the area for a suitable site. Then, satisfied, they began erecting the large orange frame tent. This they managed expertly clipping in four "bedrooms", two on either side of the centre area.

They stood back, and critically inspected their new office and hotel. Then they returned to the supplies piled on the beach and collected the equipment to furnish the tent.

Albert helped them carry stack after stack of law books and box files. Then the folding tables, chairs, cooking stoves, pots, water tanks and lanterns. He wondered where the food was.

"What's wrong?" Rhodes asked, in sudden concern.

"I was wondering where the grub is. We haven't eaten all day."

The solicitor pointed at a small packing case marked *s.s. Orcadia* "not wanted on voyage". It stood between two large crates of gin.

Then he turned back to setting up the tables, and arranging the typewriter, lamps and books.

Collins behaved as though he had worked, all his life, in a bright orange tent on a rocky islet.

His tanned, bald head shone in the warm evening sunlight as he tied a brass nameplate to a piece of driftwood he wedged into a crevice in the rock outside the tent door. "Jas. Rhodes, LL.B. Lon., Solicitor, Commissioner for Oaths." Finally, he walked back to the ski-boat, returning a few moments later with a large doormat which he laid formally in front of the tent. It read WELCOME.

Victoria found herself in the kitchen. She was surprisingly competent, and within a few minutes had set up a two-burner gas stove behind the tent.

The crackling sound of frying steak and onions was drowned by a wild thrashing noise. A helicopter, flying at little more than sea level, slashed through the air over the Island and hovered over the *Ayat*. It hung there, and they watched a small figure lower itself onto the deck of the Russian ship.

The helicopter stayed motionless for a second, then veered away, disappearing back towards the French coast.

"D'you think they've called in the top brass, sir?" Collins asked. Rhodes shrugged. He lifted his red wig and scratched his scalp.

The sky was now almost purple. Rhodes lit a gas lantern and he and Collins sat together in their office, riffling through papers from the files, consulting their books, and sipping gin.

Albert collected the cushions from the speedboat and he and Victoria sat outside the tent, watching the winking lights of the Russian Fleet. From the stranded trawler, fifty yards away, they could hear a balalaika. It was sad and melancholy. There was no breeze. The sea was motionless.

Occasionally the clatter of feet on steel ladders drummed across from the ship but they could see no movement.

At last, tired, Victoria and Albert went into the tent. She gave Albert's hand a squeeze, kissed her father, and disappeared into one of the sleeping compartments. Albert hesitated for a second, then chose the one next to her. Rhodes and Collins worked on.

Albert sat on the edge of the camp bed and watched Victoria's shadow as she undressed on the other side of the thin cotton walls. He stripped, lay back and wriggled his way down into the sleeping bag, then called her softly. A bulge showed in the wall. He reached out and managed to hold her hand on the other side of the cloth. . . .

Albert drew his bronze dagger and with a fluid movement cut through the wall of the Emperor's tent. He shook back the red plume of his helmet. His princess recognised him in the dim firelight, and gasped. He signalled her to keep silent, then beckoned her to follow him.

As they stepped into the sand outside the tent the armoured figure of a Legionary hurtled out of the darkness, a war axe twisting above its head. Albert sidestepped before the warrior could bring the blade flashing downwards. A quick thrust severed the man's carotid artery. He fell to the sand with barely a sound. Blood sank into the desert. Albert leapt onto his white stallion, then lifted the naked Victoria up behind him. The horse sprang forward, mane flying, hooves muffled. Behind, came sounds of the awakening encampment. Only voices followed them into the Egyptian night. Alone, at his secret oasis, they made love. . . .

Albert now stood in a jungle clearing, an M.16 wedged against his hip. He sprayed death at the retreating bandits. The monsoon was at its height. Warm rain threw itself against his face, blinding him and making it difficult for him to breathe . . . Victoria was calling him to her. He awoke, suddenly, to find himself still soaked and Victoria standing above him, an empty beaker in her hand. . . .

"Sorry about that," she said. "I couldn't wake you. And breakfast is ready. I've been up for over an hour."

Much of that time had been spent on personal grooming. Her father had brought her make-up case over from St Mary's, and she had made full use of it. She was wearing a sleeveless dress that Albert felt was more suitable for a cocktail party than a few days' camping.

"Daddy thinks the Russians will be over in a few minutes. You'd better get dressed."

Albert sorted through his suitcase, and found underpants and shorts. They were far more comfortable on his still burnt backside than the Russian seaman's dungarees of the past thirty-six hours. He walked through the kitchen-opening of the tent and found that Victoria had already filled him a basin of water. He washed and shaved. Then returned to tidy up his sleeping quarters and find himself a shirt. It felt good to be clean and tidy again. He didn't like dirt.

Rhodes and Collins sat together under the sun awning at the front of the tent, drinking breakfast. Albert joined them.

"Gin or cornflakes?" asked Rhodes. "We've both been up all night." He looked tired. His wig had shifted position again, and the parting now ran from ear to ear. "There's nothing like breakfast outdoors on a summer morning, even if you haven't seen your bed."

Albert chose cornflakes. The sun was already high over the Island. Towards the north, the view from the tent was almost Mediterranean. To the east it looked like a Clydeside dockyard. To the south-west, where the Russian fleet was moored, like the Spithead Review.

Albert crouched by the sea, scouring the frying pan with a handful of grit and seaweed. He heard footsteps behind him, turned, and saw Tanya approaching.

He watched her. Her uniform was freshly pressed, her hair drawn back tightly behind her ears. Black stockings and flat-heeled shoes. Albert thought she seemed as much out of place on an island as Victoria. Even so, she was attractive. Albert wondered how the two girls would look if they exchanged clothes.

" 'Ello," she said. She wasn't sure whether she should have said "Goot morging," or "Goot morden."

45

Albert's answer increased her confusion. " 'Morning," he said.

"A grand camping horse you have here, I see," she said, pointing at the tent.

Albert was startled. Then realised she meant "house".

He smiled at her.

She spoke softly.

"Captain Vorolokov says he wish speaking to you soon. He and the other officers march to the camping horse together in one hour."

Albert invited her to stay for a coffee.

"Thank you, no. Captain Vorolokov said I must quickly give you massage, and disappear."

Albert bit his lip. She turned and crunched her way over the pebbles towards the trawler.

"Do you fancy her?" a voice asked. Victoria was standing by the kitchen-opening of the tent.

"She's not a blonde, and she thinks I'm Aladdin's magic lamp," he said.

Victoria grinned. "I was listening. If she touches you, I'll massage *her*—with a rock."

Albert climbed up to the tent, and poked his head into the office.

"The Russians will be here in an hour," he said.

"We're ready for them," came the reply. "Come in and we'll tell you what we think it's best to do."

There was a clink of glass as Rhodes poured his elevenses. He pushed across a box of cigarettes. Then his desk lighter.

"We've got to start this off in a businesslike way. Anyone like a drink?"

He looked at Albert, who shook his head.

"As there's so much money involved, I'd like you to sign this agreement. Read it carefully. It authorises me to act for you in this matter. It also guarantees me five per cent. This is less than my normal percentage. But both Collins and myself feel it's sufficient for the work involved."

Rhodes downed his third gin of the day, and automatically adjusted his wig.

Albert studied the document. It seemed straightforward. He signed.

46

"Now," said Rhodes, "I suggest we try to lease, not sell, part of the Island to the Russians. They're only interested in keeping people away from that trawler. We'll tell them they can't have it for less than ninety-nine years."

A smug look spread over his face, and he poured himself another gin.

"They'll want to get the boat off as quickly as possible."

"I'll leave it completely in your hands, Mr Rhodes."

"Fine."

Victoria handed Albert a coffee, and the three men went outside and waited for their Soviet visitors.

They watched Vorolokov swing down the trawler's rope ladder and make his way to a small jetty of rocks.

The sound of the *Ayat's* cutter grew louder as it rounded the tip of the Island and headed towards Vorolokov.

He caught the painter and pulled the boat close to the rocks. Nevskii and a fresh-faced young man in a neat brown suit, carrying a briefcase, climbed ashore.

The three Russians stood near the water's edge, talking. Then they walked towards the tent.

"Are you going to need me?" Albert asked.

"No, only for a signature on the lease. But don't go far. I'll call you in when I want you. Victoria, I'd like you to keep making us lots of coffee."

The Russians smiled at Victoria and Albert as the couple stepped out of the tent.

"Please go in," said Albert.

The visitors were met by Collins who, very formally, led them to Rhodes, seated behind his desk. He stood up, and shook hands with the three men.

Nevskii introduced the stranger.

"This is Comrade Gregore Lazarev, from our Embassy in Paris."

Albert sat in the shade at the back of the tent, away from the heat of the gas stove. Victoria ran a shuttle-service of coffee cups between the kitchen and the conference.

"Now they're drinking gin in there," she told him two hours later. From where he sat, Albert could hear nothing of the negotiations going on inside. But from beneath the flap, wisps of cigar smoke leaked out.

Finally, with a flourish, the kitchen flap was pulled back and Collins poked his head out. "You're on," he said.

Inside, the air was so loaded with smoke that Albert had difficulty keeping his eyes open.

Through the haze he was introduced to Lazarev.

Rhodes put a hand on Albert's shoulder and asked him to sign the contract lying on the table. Albert caught an almost imperceptible wink. He noticed that for the first time Rhodes was not wearing his wig. He was using it to dust cigar ash off his desk. Albert took the pen and signed.

"Excellent, gentlemen," said Rhodes. He passed the newly signed document across to Lazarev. The Russian opened his briefcase and pulled out a wad of blue papers. He sorted through them, and selected one.

"Please type the gentleman's name here," he said to Collins.

Then he took it back, examined it carefully and handed it to Albert.

"Yours," he said with a smile. "We will cable our Swiss bank immediately. The money will be transferred to an account for you tomorrow."

Lazarev bowed to Victoria, shook hands with the three men and walked out of the tent. The two others said farewell and left.

For thirty yards the Russians walked, slowly, without exchanging a word. Then Nevskii nudged Vorolokov in the ribs and playfully punched Lazarev on the shoulder. "Our new colony. Easy as falling overboard," the new Admiral said. There were suppressed chuckles. The three men linked arms and gleefully humming the Internationale strode briskly towards the cutter, and the already planned celebration aboard the *Ayat*.

Albert was still looking at the piece of blue paper in his hand. It was in French.

"What does it mean," he asked.

"It means, my boy, you're a millionaire. One and a half times over. Let me be the first to congratulate you. Have a gin."

Victoria hugged Albert. She decided she loved millionaires. Collins had disappeared. He was back seconds later holding a bottle of Graves in one hand, and balancing a tray of four glasses on the other.

"Sorry, no champagne. Let's celebrate."

Albert was dazed.

They had lunch, then Rhodes and Collins met the Russian survey party to mark the dividing line across the Island. Albert and Victoria watched as a broad white stripe was painted from water's edge to water's edge the width of Foul Rock.

"Somehow, I feel sad about that," said Albert. "That was the part of the Island that I liked best. It's where I met you."

In London, S.W.1, a tired and harassed senior British decoding officer telephoned the Prime Minister.

"Priority. Sir, the Russians are buying an Island in the Channel."

There was a long silence.

"Hello, sir, did you hear me?"

A calm voice came over the wire. "Would you mind repeating that?"

"The Russians, sir, are buying an Island. Just off the Scillies."

"My goodness!" said the P.M. "I'm supposed to start my holiday there next week. Got any details?"

"They're sketchy. All we know is that it's a privately owned Island, outside territorial waters. We've never claimed it. There are Russian warships all round it."

"Send in the Home Fleet," ordered the P.M.

There was a pause.

"What d'you mean she's booked for Sunday?"

There was another pause.

"Philip who? I don't care if he is the admiral's nephew ... *Whose* husband?"

There was a third, briefer, pause.

"Oh, him!" grumbled the P.M. "I bet he wouldn't lend us *Bluebottle* if he wanted her for Cowes Week." He slammed down the receiver.

A red telephone standing beside the Hot Line teleprinter on his right buzzed aggressively. He picked it up. An American voice boomed across three thousand miles:

"Well, have you stopped it?"

"I don't think we can. But I'll try after lunch."

"That'll be too goddamned late," the voice screamed. There was a pause, then, "How's your good lady?"

The P.M. heard the click of the receiver being replaced at the White House.

"Very well, thanks," he snarled into the dead instrument.

5

Albert lay, sticky in his sleeping bag, a dribble of sweat ran down onto his stomach. He rubbed it.

It was stifling in the tent. Someone had closed the doors and there was no ventilation. Collins was snoring. Victoria was lying against the separating wall. With his hand Albert could feel the roundness of her bottom. She moved at his touch.

He reached down to the tent floor and searched for his cigarettes. One of the legs of the bed rested on the packet. He pulled it free, then tore it open. Most of the cigarettes were damaged. He found a good one, and lit it.

In the flare of the burning match he looked at his watch. It was nearly four o'clock, and still dark.

The sound of a distant helicopter had awakened him. It grew louder.

"Who the hell's coming now?" he wondered. "Trying to sleep here is like kipping in a fairground."

The noise swelled. A light flashed across the tent roof. In panic Albert thought the aircraft was going to crash on top of them. The tent flapped and thrashed. The canvas wall smacked him sharply in the back. The light blazed again. He slid out of the sleeping bag, off his camp bed and dashed outside.

With a squelch from its rubber floats, the helicopter dropped onto the plateau, only thirty yards away. Its search-light cut through the darkness and blinded him, pinning him in its beam. He covered his eyes with his hands. The light was so strong, he could still see a pink glow.

The engine died. The light moved off him. He took his hands away, but could see only psychedelic patterns. His ears throbbed.

51

Someone got hold of his arm. He jumped.

"Who is it?" asked Victoria.

"It's me," he said.

"I meant out there, you idiot."

Rhodes and Collins stood beside them, dressed in their pyjamas. Rhodes' wig was propped up by his left eyebrow.

The searchlight was aimed past them, to the side of the tent. A tall, camouflaged combat suit loped into the saucer of light. It was carrying a valise under one arm. A quick-draw holster was strapped cowboy-style low on one thigh. On the left breast of the jacket was a large label "Polyanski".

"Who's Quinlan?" asked the figure, spitting the word past the gnarled stub of a cheroot.

The demand was so military that Albert almost leapt to attention.

"It's me."

Collins sparked the gas lantern into life inside the tent, and Rhodes led the way in. The tall figure stooped to get through the doorway. He was at least six foot six. He looked down at them, his long arms moving loosely. He unstrapped his helmet and tossed it into a corner.

"Guess you know what I've come about."

"You want to back out of the deal?" queried Albert, nervously eyeing the label on the jacket, and mentally watching a million or so winged pound notes fluttering away.

"Deal?"

"Who are you?" asked Rhodes.

"Sorry, fellas, Nathan Polyanski, General, U.S. Marine Corp, attached to the Sixth Fleet."

"I thought you were Russian," said Albert. "Y'know. The name." He poked sheepishly at the label.

"A glass of gin, sir, or coffee?" Collins looked at the visitor wearily. He thought of Mrs Collins, warmly tucked in bed back on the Scillies. He didn't like getting up as early as this.

Rhodes spoke: "If you've come about the Russians, I'm afraid you're too late. We've already signed a contract with them. They've got half of the island, and there's . . .

The General interrupted. "We know about that. It's this

part we want. I'll make the deal here and now. What's your price?"

Rhodes looked at Albert, and back at the General.

"Why do you want it?"

General Polyanski eased himself onto one of the canvas chairs. It was so low that his long legs doubled up like a grasshopper's. He pushed them out across the tent. Pulling a new cheroot out of his pocket, he lit it before replying.

"We've monitored all the Russian signals. You've been fooled. You may think the Ruskies want to get their boat off the Island. But they don't. They want this place as a listening post. I guess you couldn't know how important Foul Rock is to them. They have us checked." He spat a tobacco stem. "We're in a mess. That's why we've got to have the other half of the Island. Somehow or other we wanna plug their ears with a jamming station."

Rhodes was embarrassed.

"We thought they would just salvage their trawler. I didn't expect them to be here for more than a few weeks."

"Right," said the General. "We'll pay you the same amount as the Russians. Dollars, of course. We'd like immediate possession."

"How immediate?" asked Rhodes.

"Like now."

There was a cough from Collins. "I believe we can use the lease I was preparing for your cottage on the mainland, Mr Rhodes. It's a little irregular, but we can make alterations and it'll be quicker than drawing up fresh documents."

Collins found the lease in one of the files.

"There are a number of clauses I'm sure you will agree to."

"Let's hear them," said the General.

"Naturally, we would expect no sub-letting."

The General smiled.

"I don't suppose you'll be using the Island for immoral purposes, the commercial boarding of domestic animals, or for breeding maggots for fishing bait?"

The General's smile became a grin.

Collins continued in his flat, legal voice. "Normally, we'd insist that no radios be played after 11 p.m., and that tenants be God-fearing and attend church regularly. We can, however, dispense with the radio clause and those that relate to the condition of the roof thatch, the pollution of the well and all reference to the regular servicing of the cess-pit."

The General laughed. Collins ignored the interruption.

"Clause seven must be adhered to. The landlord, or his representative, shall have free access. And we'll amend clause eight, which says prior to the termination of the lease, the property must be restored to its original condition, repainted and given three coats of best quality clear varnish."

"Boy," said the General. "Congress'll wet their pants when they hear the terms. Leave the roof bit in. I'll love telling 'em that America's 51st State'll have to be rethatched."

Albert signed and doubled his wealth.

The General looked at his watch and stood up. "Got to get back to the fleet. We'll have our men here soon," he said briskly. "Been great doing business with you. Maybe I can get a few days' fishing here later."

Collins opened the door of the tent to let out the visitor. He gasped. The clerk rarely coloured his language. He did now.

"Jesus Christ! Look!" He pointed across towards the eastern end of the Island.

In the thin light of the dawn, they saw the barrier. It stretched across the Rock. A Berlin Wall, eight feet high. It consisted of coils of barbed wire, supported on pyramids of pointed steel stakes. Midway along was a high gate of barbed wire. Behind it stood a newly-built tower fifteen feet high. On the platform at the top a man was sitting — behind a machine-gun. Above him hung a searchlight.

At the gate stood a dark figure, cradling a machine-pistol. He held a guard dog on a short chain leash.

"What did you expect?" asked the General.

They stepped outside the tent. A small group of Russians watched from beside the raised rocket on the deck of the *Dmitri Kirov* as the helicopter took off and disappeared.

"I come here for a holiday. I make three million quid, and I can't get a decent night's sleep," Albert told Victoria. "We'd get more peace in a saw mill."

There was no point in going back to bed.

Albert and Victoria stood and watched the Russians behind the wire. They waved to Vorolokov on the deck of the trawler. He pretended not to see them. They strolled over to the wire fence. The dog pulled at its lead. The Russian on the watchtower sat rigid behind his machine-gun. The guard with the dog hefted his machine-pistol. The atmosphere was too uncomfortable. They walked back to the tent.

"They're ruining our lovely Island," said Victoria. "Do you think there's going to be trouble when the Americans arrive?"

"We'll soon know," replied Albert. "Look out there."

He pointed to the west. Black against the sky-line was a war fleet: cruisers, destroyers, two aircraft-carriers. Between the Island and the fleet were smaller ships. They were racing so fast that even though they were still far away, white waves could be seen breaking from their bows.

"Let's get back to the others."

The four of them stood together on the plateau, watching the ships speeding towards them. Above was a helicopter —larger than any they had seen before. With two huge rotors, one at either end, it shepherded the vessels.

The sight was frightening. As the ships drew nearer, a landing craft broke away from them. The helicopter whirled ahead and stationed itself on the approach to the Island. Its doors opened. Inside, crouching khaki figures held carbines. There was a huge white star on the fuselage with the words "U.S. Marine Corps".

As it reached the shallows, the bow door of the landing craft dropped. Rows of grim-faced figures knelt—helmeted, clutching automatic rifles. Albert could see a grenade held in the hands of the leader. With a crash the boat hit the rocks and shovelled into a small bay.

"Geronimo!"

The boyish Marine Lieutenant holding the grenade glanced back over his shoulder. It was his great moment. He waved the men to follow him.

"Geronimo!" he screamed again.

The American assault troops leapt onto the beach and hit the pebbles at a run. The leaders jumped for the protection

55

of the first row of rocks below the startled Britons.

As they menaced the ground ahead with their weapons, the second wave of men surged forward.

"Charge!"

The Americans leapt from cover to cover until they were level with the orange tent.

"Mornin' Ma'am," called the young Lieutenant to Victoria, as he ran past in the direction of the Russians. He was still holding the grenade.

"Spread out and hit dirt," he yelled. The landing party fanned across the island and dived for whatever shelter they could find. Their rifles pointed ahead at the two Russian seamen who stared, disbelievingly.

"Dig in."

There was a clang as fifteen shovels hit hard rock at the same time.

"He must be kiddin'," drawled a voice.

"Morelli, do up your flies, there's a dame here," said another.

The helicopter had swung away. There was silence.

"Radio," shouted a red-faced Major who knelt near the tent. A heavily loaded figure with a long aerial sprouting from the box on its back wriggled across the plateau on its stomach, until it reached the officer.

"Call 'em in," ordered the Major.

"Red Member to Eager Mary. Red Member to Eager Mary. Are you receiving me? Over."

Victoria raised her eyebrows.

The Major looked at her. "I'll kill the guy who thought up these code names," he said.

"Red Member in position. Red Member in position. It's all yours. Out."

The supply fleet, which had been circling a few hundred yards off the island, turned and headed in until the boats were lined, side by side, bows to the rocks. More of the camouflaged figures jumped ashore and formed human chains, passing dozens of boxes, until they were piled high all along the rocks, and stretched up to the plateau.

No one paid any attention to the orange tent or its occupants.

A team from one of the boats brought in large pieces of

what looked like a cannon and began building it on the flat piece of rock immediately in front of the gate to the Russian sector.

The Russian fishermen stood stupified. The two guards were joined by the remainder of the trawler's crew, and the scientists. They lined the barbed wire fence and watched the landing in astonishment.

The mysterious "cannon" was slowly taking shape. It seemed to consist of a series of large diameter pipes, fastened together into one square section. At last, a number of long boxes were opened and finned projectiles were fed down into the tubes in its main section.

"Good God," said Rhodes, "a rocket launcher."

At last, satisfied, the engineers who had built the battery called over the red-faced officer. With exaggerated ceremony, he ranged the weapon onto its target some forty yards away . . . the *Dmitri Kirov*.

While it was being assembled, the scene on the American sector of the Island was like a disturbed anthill. Figures hurried in all directions as they went about their mysterious jobs.

Sections of sheet plastic, tarpaulin, canvas, coils of rope, long baulks of timber were rushed about. The four Britons occasionally recognised familiar shapes . . . doors, window frames, chemical toilets, chairs, a piano, even a Coca-Cola dispenser.

As they watched, a garrison town grew on the rocky ground.

Their orange tent became the corner-stone for rows of pup tents forming two sides of a barracks square on the plateau.

Miniature sentry boxes dominated the south edge of the island, behind the larger of two prefabricated buildings.

Victoria gazed wonderingly at them. She was about to ask the question when a Marine hammered a sign into a crack in the rocks. It said "Latrines".

Other signs began appearing. The larger of the two buildings was labelled "The Silver Dollar". A board, over the entrance, said "Mess—and we ain't foolin'."

The other building wore the sign "PX Store—U.S. Military Personnel Only".

Only one wigwam-shaped structure remained unnamed. But its greasy sides and the smoke already drifting from its entrance speedily identified it as the cookhouse.

The smoke snaked over the figures of the armed Marines still lying prostrate in front of the now-amused Russians behind their barbed wire.

A dozen Vostok cameras clicked, as the trawlermen chronicled the scene. Their watch-tower bent sideways as eager figures climbed up the ladder to the already crowded platform to view the panorama.

Vorolokov sat on the edge of the *Dmitri Kirov's* bow, swinging his legs and smoking one of his dark cigarettes. Tanya stood at his shoulder.

A quarter of a mile off-shore, the sun bounced back from the lenses of binoculars as the crew of the Russian supply ship *Ayat* watched.

One solitary figure ignored the invasion, and the turmoil which followed. He sat on the rock normally occupied by the cormorants, holding a length of cord in his hand. It was Boris, the trawler cook. He was completely absorbed in his work, fishing. A bucket at his side was overflowing with pollack.

He hauled the line in, baited it carefully with a piece of bacon, and lobbed it back into the sea with a splash. Having missed the invasion, he was also unaware of the withdrawal of the Marines' engineers.

The Island was suddenly calm again as the landing craft pulled away.

The red-faced American Major stood beneath the flagpole erected in the centre of the plateau. The assault section still lay motionless close to the Russian barrier.

"Fall in," he shouted.

There was a scramble as the Marines got to their feet and doubled to the square around the flagpole.

The young Ensign, who had bravely led the "attack", snapped forward and saluted the Major.

"The Colours," he was told.

He opened his combat jacket and unreeled the Stars and Stripes which he'd wrapped round his skeletal figure.

He clipped them to the halyard, and waited for the Major's order.

"Field Music Bugler."

A Marine took two paces and pulled a bugle from his pack. With a flourish he swung it to his lips.

Across the island the harsh military notes chipped the windless air.

The Ensign hoisted the flag.

It hung there, limp.

To the simple Russian fisherman, it was an emotional moment. From behind the wire barrier came an involuntary cheer. Tanya clapped.

"For Chrrrrist's sake, Morelli, fasten your flies," said a voice.

The Americans had arrived.

Meanwhile, back in London, the Prime Minister was answering the telephone.

"Priority, sir. The Americans are buying half an island in the Channel."

There was a long silence.

"Hello, sir. Did you hear me?"

A tremulous voice answered him. "Which half of which island?"

"The one the Russians have the other half of."

"What the hell's going on there? Find out. And quick."

He put down the 'phone as the Hot Line buzzed.

"Washington?" he asked.

"Non, Paris. Will you accept a reverse charge call?"

"Ha! Ha! Tres amusing," the P.M. said, assuming his Merseyside French accent. "If it's about the Island, we're trying to stop them."

"As usual, you've not outed ze finger to shift ze ass. You're too late," said the caller. "How's Madame?"

The P.M. tried to race the descending French receiver.

"Tres bon, thanks," he snorted into the dead instrument.

6 Rainwater gurgled under the built-in groundsheet of the orange tent, and escaped in confused skeins down the side of the plateau towards the beach. The barrack square was an inland sea. The flag wrapped wetly around its pole. Spray from the heavy rain leapt, in a mist, a foot above the rocks. The tents sparkled.

The Russian guard, sitting on the tower in a shelter formed by a piece of tarpaulin hung over the searchlight, looked down in satisfaction at the saturated American sentry below. Rain sluiced off the Marine's helmet and ran down his neck beneath his oilskins. He stood motionless, watching the Russian trawler. His jaws were stiffened on a pad of chewing gum. The barrel of his carbine protruded from his cape and pissed a waterfall onto his combat boots.

The Foul Rock crisis jolted the world's Press through the chatter of teleprinters. It was the day after the American landing. The teletype machine at the London *Daily Express* stuttered, and stopped in the middle of a sentence. The bell signalled an important message. It hammered back to life. It was midnight. A tape-room messenger shoved his well-fingered *Lady Chatterley* into his pocket and tore the paper from the teleprinter. He carried it to a telephone-cluttered desk.

The Night Foreign Editor was thin and always hungry. He sat at the desk, eating his third dinner of the shift. The messenger waved the bulletin between the ascending forkful of pie and the NFE's face. He was so absorbed in his food that he half speared the message into his mouth.

"Would yer like me to put it between bread for yer?" asked the messenger. He ran a lucrative sideline selling drug store commodities to the night staff. "Want any stainless razor-blades while I'm 'ere?"

"No, thanks, Ginge. I've had closer shaves from your French letters. I'll have a fag, though."

"Bugger off," said Ginge.

"Bloody Hell. . . ."

The NFE planted his fork into a pile of mashed potato and rushed the message across the open-plan room to the night editor's desk with its covering of page proofs.

"Got your splash—a good one from New York. Russians and Americans have each got half an island off the Scillies. Russians accusing the Yanks in the United Nations of aggression. I'll ask New York for more."

The *Express* immediately front-paged its new crusade. It called for a referendum of the Island's inhabitants. Let them choose, it shouted, by free vote whether they want British, Russian or American rule. As usual, it called on the British Prime Minister to resign.

The reactions of other London newspapers were also characteristic.

The *Daily Mail* launched a win-a-car competition, asking entrants to place in order of preference ten most unlikely items it said would be essential for life on an island.

The *Sun,* in an editorial backing the housewives' plight, slammed the American occupation of Foul Rock, for the effect it would have on the cost of living in the U.S. half.

The *Sketch* headlines read: "They're protecting an island like this." The entire front page, below the type, was a photograph of a bikini-clad girl sitting on a rock.

The *Daily Mirror* banner declared: Missile threat to Island's wildlife.

The *Telegraph* dug into its files and produced the report of an ornithologist who visited the Island in 1889. It published the fact that marsh gas seeped through the rocks. "Mineral bonanza," reasoned the newspaper.

The Times filled its inside pages with interpretive assessments by its various experts. It also carried other news that morning. But not very much.

The Guardian, on the other hand, just published other news. They'd make up for it the following day.

The newspapers went to war.

By 1 a.m. the beagles of Fleet Street, the foreign newsmen, and television and radio teams were on their way. The West Country staff correspondents had already been alerted by their news desk to "get to Foul Rock fastest." But they needed reinforcements for major projection of the story. Telephones rang in late-night restaurants, homes, and the Press Club. Halves of bitter, gins and tonic, wives and girl friends were abandoned. Reporters, on and off duty, were dragged back, some happy, some protesting, to their offices. They were briefed, and despatched.

An agitated pressman dashed from his office, ran a gauntlet of taxis, occupied by the opposition, as he made for his MGB. He peeled a ticket for "parking without lights" off his windscreen and stuck it on the front of a rival newspaper van. Then he accelerated away, tyres squeaking.

Now, for everyone, the target was—be first there, and get the news back.

Half an hour after the alert, there were no charter planes available south of Manchester.

Big money changed ownership. Photographers, pregnant with camera-gear, lumbered into aircraft.

Reporters who barely an hour earlier had broken off their story-swapping in the Press Club, resumed it at the airport and railway station buffets. On the A30, police patrol cars had a busy time pursuing a column of fast cars speeding westward.

Not all those who set off arrived. There were calamities and casualties.

For the airborne, there were dramas. A Scots reporter had uncorked a half-bottle of red wine in the Press Club just as he was called back to his office. He tucked it into the inside breast pocket of his suit as he left. There it stayed, forgotten. His evening's drinking and the bumpy flight made him abruptly leave his companions. He leant over the low bowl to be sick. The forgotten bottle of wine spilled over his shirt.

He left the lavatory and staggered back up the gangway.

"Mother of God," said the voice of a devout Irish television personality. "Simon's cut his bloody throat."

The stewardess, who was exchanging telephone numbers with a young journalist, looked up and fainted. The journalist spent the rest of the flight giving her the kiss of life.

A noisy poker school was claiming the newspapermen's expense allowances on another flight.

One of the players, with an eye on the time, stood up to leave after a winning hand.

"Give us a chance to win it back."

"Sorry," he said. "But I've got work to do."

"That's no excuse. There's nothing to write. You can't send anything back from here."

"I'm not trying to get anything back. I'm trying to get it there. I'm the pilot."

Seven flushed faces drained white.

By dawn, most of the journalists were in Cornwall. Some had arrived from France, Belgium, Holland and Germany. But one party from London, who scrounged a lift on a fast goods train carrying a cargo of bullion, found themselves shunted into a siding. They were rescued three hours later by a posse of police searching for the mislaid gold.

It was like market day in Penzance.

Newsmen, who had been unable to charter light aircraft to take them direct to the Scilly Isles, hunted for transport. The helicopter service to St Mary's on the Scillies had already been doubled and the first machine left at dawn.

Fishing boats, loaded with reporters and cameramen, were already at sea. Still hung-over, exhausted from lack of sleep, hungry and now sea-sick, they heaved their way towards Foul Rock.

It was raining, miserable and windy. As the boats left the shelter of the Cornish coast, they were hit by a squall. They dipped and corkscrewed into a south-westerly.

The passengers flipped coins for spare oilskins and for the shelter of the smelly for'ard cabins.

Many of those whose stomachs survived the waves couldn't withstand the smell of fish, sweat and diesel fumes.

A miserable, anoraked figure doubled over the rail. "Abide with me," he moaned, tunelessly.

"But they only sing that at sea disasters and at the Cup Final. And I can't see any footballers," said his sympathetic colleague, holding him by the belt.

63

"Do me a favour. Push me in."

The Cornish fisherman in the wheelhouse laughed. They chewed on their pipes and swigged at bottles of brown ale. By their standards, this was mild weather.

The wind dropped. The rain increased. Visibility was less than a mile. The journey seemed endless. The sea was now beaten flat.

The first journalists reached Foul Rock at 9 a.m. They were French, a team from *Paris-Match*, on board a large off-shore racing launch, straight from Cherbourg.

The French power-boat arrived unnoticed and dropped anchor. A rubber dinghy was lowered over the side, and poled to the rocks. The first of the journalists stepped onto the Island.

"Halt, stand-where-yer-are." The Marine guard whirled into a fighting crouch, his carbine at his hip. He spat out his chewing gum. "What d'ya want?"

"We'd like to speak to the Commandant. We're from *Paris-Match*."

The Marine wrenched at his lanyard and produced a whistle. He blew three short blasts. The Mess emptied as men ran to their posts.

The visitors weren't made welcome. Red-faced Major Corrigan grudgingly spoke to them. He said "no comment." He didn't object to photographs. No, he wouldn't pose with a Russian guard, nor on his own.

The Marines went back to their Mess, leaving the five Frenchmen standing on the shore in the rain. They tried a similar approach to the Russians at the gate, but were ignored.

The cameramen photographed all they could see on the Island.

They were reloading when they spotted the half-dressed Victoria standing at the door of the orange tent.

"Merde, alors. Sex."

Within seconds the tent was full of lusting Frenchmen.

The flotilla of Press then hit Foul Rock. The guard's whistle shrilled again as the boats appeared through the drizzle.

The Russians reacted firmly. Storm-clad armed guards

slid down the rope ladder from the trawler and stationed themselves on the rocks.

There was a loud bang, and a red flare hung above the trawler. The robot tones of a loudhailer reached the journalists over the sounds of their boats' engines.

"Attention. Keep away. Keep away. You cannot land here. You are in Soviet territorial waters. Move out."

"And balls to you, Ivan," shouted the Cockney voice of a cameraman. There was loud, coarse laughter.

Obediently, however, the boats turned to the American end of the Island. They nudged each other for moorings. Cautious fishermen were bribed into getting their boats closer. There was a scramble to get ashore.

The next few minutes were profitable for the German and Japanese camera industries. In the scuffle, a cameraman slipped on wet fish scales in one of the boats, and landed, face forward, in a belly-flop. The lens was punched into his camera's body. A journalist jumped from boat to boat to reach shore. He clutched at a camera-festooned photographer. Both men disappeared into the sea. They were gaffed back on board by the skilled crew of a shark-fishing boat.

A television cameraman, hand-holding a £1,700 Arriflex, leapt ashore, tripped over a mooring rope and took three uncontrolled strides up the rocks. The camera tore itself from the battery lead and trajected fifteen feet into the air.

It soared through the open top of one of the latrines. It landed with a splash.

Boats continued to arrive. It was still raining.

"For God's sake, Collins, hide the gin." Rhodes sat inside the tent door, watching the advancing pressmen.

The *Paris-Match* crew were photographing Victoria and Albert against the background of the trawler. Suddenly, they were avalanched by shoving, elbowing, shutter-clicking rivals. Albert found himself behind the mass.

"A bit more leg, love."

She was wearing a white shirt knotted above her naval and a faded blue denim hipster-mini. Her swamped yellow hair clung to her neck. Her shirt was almost transparent in the rain. She was bra-less.

"Take a deep breath."

"Can we have that button undone?" A hand was slapped away.

"Look up."

"Stretch."

"Lean towards me."

"Say 'moon'."

The American Marines, who had turned out to watch Victoria modelling, found themselves surrounded by questioning newspapermen.

There was no shelter from the rain for the journalists. The Americans were adamant. No non-military personnel were allowed in their tents or Mess.

"Sorry, fellas, we can't even accommodate half of you," the Major told them.

People were almost falling off the edge of the Island, and more were arriving every minute.

Newsmen milled against the barbed wire as they tried to interview the Russians. The Soviet seamen were getting nervous and jittery.

Major Corrigan tried to find his Lieutenant in the crowd. It was impossible. He couldn't even find a Marine to ask him to find the Lieutenant. He forced his way to his communications tent, and called the Fleet carrier.

"Get them off, and keep them off," he was told.

He tried shouting. He was ignored. He tried pushing, but there were too many—and they pushed back.

The journalists hadn't eaten or drunk for several hours. Then someone found the Coca-Cola machine. A black-market rapidly developed in American dimes. Morelli, flies open, found the pocketful of dimes he'd won at poker the previous night was worth a fortune. He'd cornered the market.

It was the Russians who solved the Americans' over-crowding problem. A combination of the Soviet seamen and the Cockney cameraman.

Trying for an exclusive fraternisation picture, the Cockney lobbed a Coca-Cola tin up to the Russian on the watch-tower. The guard recoiled in horror, and kicked the tin in the direction of the sea. He shouted a warning.

His comrade below thought it was a grenade, and threw himself flat on the ground. He lobbed back a teargas bomb.

66

The guard on the tower accidentally triggered off a short burst into the air. The teargas bomb rolled beneath the cook-house tent and hissed.

There was silence. Then, from inside the tent, came a yelp of fury from Zeke, the barefooted Kentucky cook who was drying his boots in the oven.

He hopped to the tent door, clutching a handful of bruised toes, eyes burning.

Elliot M. Hennessey, the coloured Top-Sergeant, tossed him a carbine. Zeke grabbed at the wrong half of the double-image he saw through his tears. The carbine slammed him in the chest, then dropped onto his undamaged foot. He collapsed, a set of swelling toes in each fist.

"Ya goddam Irish bastard. I'm sick an' tired of your stupid tricks."

"What you want, a Purple Heart?" asked the Sergeant.

The American Grunts had grabbed their weapons. The journalists saw the Marines' friendly faces go hard and war-like.

Major Corrigan shouted to his men: "Get these jerks out of here. We've a shoot-out on our hands."

The evacuation of the journalists was even quicker than their arrival. It was instantaneous. Two minutes after the exodus began, only the lame and the sick were left, crawling in the direction of their boats. It was the start of a Grand Prix. Scars of foamed water radiated from the Island like the spokes of a wheel, as the journalists raced to get their story back.

Albert walked to the barrier, through the debris left behind by the newspapermen. The Russian guard who'd thrown the teargas stood there, explaining to Vorolokov and Ushakov.

The Russian Captain juggled the tin of Coca-Cola from one hand to the other.

"That was a bit close, wasn't it," said Albert.

"Yes," grinned Vorolokov. "And we weren't even trying."

The Prime Minister stood by the window of his office in Downing Street, trying out his new electric razor. He was shaving one of the cactus plants in the tray on the sill. He didn't hear the red telephone buzz.

He blew the cactus bristles out of the razor and examined his morning's work. Eleven green sausages stood nude in the dry sand.

The telephone rang again. This time he picked it up.

"Washington," a voice said.

"Prime Minister here."

"Like you to keep your newsmen off the Island. Strict news embargo. We're trying to de-escalate. Pulling out the Fleet today. The Russians are doing the same."

"Be a pleasure to help."

"Jesus!" gasped the voice. "Please don't help—just stay out of it."

The Prime Minister tensed himself for the inevitable question about his wife's well-being. It didn't come. The White House 'phone was already down.

The P.M. hummed distractedly and walked his fingers over the surface of the water in his goldfish bowl.

7 Mischa was lovingly fingering his balalaika when the wailing started again in the American sector. It happened at this time every evening ever since the Russian and American war fleets had left. It began as low sobs and flowered into a harsh, agonised shriek. It undulated through stratas of pain and misery.

The Russian seamen were sitting on the foredeck, their backs against the wheelhouse. They had been enjoying the mellow evening warmth. Now, their nerves, shaved to the surface by the noise, they could stand it no longer.

"The Americans are inhuman." Igor stirred the conversation. He was the youngest fisherman, a twenty-one-year-old wild Cossack. "No Cossack would treat even a Russian like that."

Boris, the cook, ignored the second half of the remark.

"Not all people have our humanity. The Americans are barely civilised. They have no cultural background."

"They're pigs." Vasili knocked his pipe out against the heel of his boot. "They not only exploit the world, but they exploit each other."

"We can't allow them to go on torturing a fellow-man like this," said Sacha.

"What do you want us to do, start another war?" asked Boris.

The distressed sobbing died away.

"Maybe they've killed him," said Igor. "It would be better if they have."

Vasili banged his fist on the deck. "If we're men, then we must do something about it."

"No good asking the Captain for help." Boris nodded in the direction of the cabin. "He'd mess it up."

"I'll rescue him," Igor boasted.

"Cossacks have less sense than their horses. We must have a good plan," said Boris. "We must get all the ordinary seamen to help. Everyone must be sworn to secrecy."

That night, the Rescue Committee met in the chain locker. It was reminiscent of the pre-1917 revolution days. Boris balanced on a coil of chain in front of a candle. Around him, in the half darkness, the flame wriggled shadows on the grim faces of the crew. The talk was in whispers.

"We have agreed then? The man must be rescued?" Boris spoke as self-elected leader.

There was a general mumble of consent.

"Then, we must do it as soon as possible. Tomorrow night, before the moon rises."

The plan was simple. Sacha and Lev would be the two sentries on watch at the American frontier. Sacha was to distract the US guard, while Lev gave the rescue party the all-clear signal. Then they would wade round the end of the wire and head for the rocky outcrop behind the smaller of the two square huts. There, they would wait until the persecuted man was released. It would be easy.

The torture procedure was always the same. The unhappy coloured American conscript, press-ganged into the US services, would disappear into a small tent. There he would be tormented. Half an hour later, he would stumble back to the hut, still wailing and sobbing.

"Now we must make our oath," directed Boris. "I will eat any man who breaks it. It is not often fishermen like us can give new life to oppressed races." The daring of the task they had set themselves made him glow inside.

It was obvious to Vorolokov the next day that something unusual was going on. He tried a few subtle enquiries. They were fruitless. He asked outright. But he still learned nothing. It wasn't mutiny: he could sense no increased resentment against himself. It wasn't desertion: precious belongings were still in their familiar places above the crew's bunks.

For the men, it was a long day. They watched the American guards change over every two hours, and tried to discover a pattern of movement—there wasn't one. The Americans walked the length of the wire whenever they felt like the exercise. The young Englishman and the pretty blonde girl swam and sunbathed as usual and were joined by the off-duty Marines. Occasionally the seaman caught glimpses of the coloured man.

The unemployed Russians spent most of their time fishing. Boris on his favourite rock, the others in a dinghy. The seamen knew it would be a long stay. Sacha was making a net. It grew rapidly and neatly, and was carefully rolled away whenever he had to go on watch.

The scientists no longer needed on the Island had left with the Soviet fleet. Only Ushakov remained, and he spent most of his time below decks, repairing and modifying the equipment, and preparing it for the important listening work ahead.

Vorolokov noticed the odd glances between men as he passed. Something was climaxing. The question was what?

That night, dinner was early. To Vorolokov's knowledge this had never happened before. He studied his crew as he sat down. He noticed an air of authority about Boris undetected before. Even the men felt it. For once, there were no coarse jibes about the food. It was all very mysterious.

Igor disappeared and came in with a bottle of vodka.

"Is it somebody's birthday?" Vorolokov watched the faces carefully as he put the question.

There was a silence.

"Why do you ask?"

"There's something going on."

There was another silence.

"It's my birthday," said three seamen simultaneously.

"What's today's date?" Vorolokov asked.

There was no reply.

"Well, it's my birthday soon. Let's drink to that and honest fishermen." Vorolokov downed half a mug of vodka.

Embarrassed, the men ate without speaking.

Vorolokov wondered whether the conspiracy had anything to do with fishing. There had been a lot of talk about the gear carried on the boats that had brought the journalists. He hoped his crew weren't planning a raid on the Scilly Islanders' lobster pots. He wanted no poaching, nor anything that could prejudice the future.

71

They were now in the unique position of living the life that they had always wanted—being paid as active military seamen, with few official duties to interfere with their fishing.

He realised he was alone. During his reverie the crew had left the tables.

Tanya came in.

"Join me in a drink. It's Igor's, Vasili's and Mischa's birthday. We're one big, conspiratorial family."

"But Igor's an orphan, and doesn't know when he was born."

"Precisely!" said Vorolokov.

They drank.

The plotters, met, again, in the darkened chain locker. They were wearing blue boiler suits and rope-soled shoes.

"Everybody here? We ready?"

Boris pulled a tobacco tin from his pocket and opened it.

He scooped out a fingerful of greasy soot collected from the galley chimney and passed the tin on in the dark.

"Use this," he said.

He smeared a coating over his face, and rubbed some onto the back of his hands. The others imitated him.

"I will kill the guards," Igor produced an eighteen-inch silver-handled Cossack knife from behind a coil of chains, and waved it savagely.

His friends fell on him.

There was a blanketed cry.

"Keep quiet in there." Josef poked his head inside the door from where he was standing guard outside. "What's going on?"

"It's Igor. He thinks he's going on an assassination."

There were curses. Thuds. And groans. Chains rattled. Something hit the steel floor with a loud clang.

"Shut up," Josef said again.

There were more thuds. And a knifeless Igor was pushed out onto the deck.

His bottom lip was already ballooned. He spat blood over the side of the ship. He was followed out by Boris, who was holding a dirty rag to his nose.

Josef watched, surprised, as the rest of the conspirators came out of the chain locker. None had escaped injury. It had been a brief battle. Igor had lived up to his claimed Cossack ancestry.

They crept to the side of the ship and lowered themselves into the darkness beneath the hull.

There was a moan.

"What's the matter," asked Boris. His voice was hushed but urgent.

"Which one of us weighs 152 pounds?" asked Vasili.

"Igor," said Igor.

"Well, move. You're on my hand."

Igor jumped the last six rungs.

There was a sound like air being forced out of a mattress.

"What now?" Boris asked.

A wheeze answered him. "Your bloody domesticated Cossack is using me as a trampoline, and he's broken my pocket watch."

"Quiet. I'll go and tell Sacha we're ready." Boris crawled away on his stomach. Ahead of him he could see Sacha and the barbed wire silhouetted against the night sky.

Boris's scalp tingled. He was back twenty-five years. The guard ahead of him was one of the men he had killed during his escape from Treblinka. His lips pulled back from his teeth. He crawled on.

Sacha was watching the American tents, awaiting Boris's arrival. When it came it was completely unexpected—and violent. He heard nor saw nothing, until a muscular arm clamped round his windpipe and forced back his head till he could hear his neck creaking. He just had time to croak "Boris", before he passed out.

He came to a few seconds later, his face wet. The cook was kneeling at his side. Warm, sooty tears rain-dropped down from Boris's miserable face.

He hugged him like a bear.

"Sacha, forgive me. I almost killed you."

"No need to explain, my friend. I have thought the same thoughts, standing here at the wire. We share bad memories."

Sacha sat up. "Are the others ready?"

Boris wiped his sleeve across his face, leaving a white path below his eyes.

"Ready," he sniffed. "Where's Lev and the dog?"

73

"He's waiting for you down by the water. I'll give you ten minutes. Then I'll get working."

Boris wormed his way back to the *Dmitri Kirov*. The others were waiting.

"Come on," he called softly. "It's time. Don't make a sound."

The black snake of figures made its way diagonally towards the water's edge and the end of the wire. They found it difficult to move quietly among the rock-pools. The tide was low. The rocks, with their coating of seaweed, were difficult to cross.

There was a sucking noise. A quiet splash.

"Who's that?" hissed Boris.

"It's Igor," said Igor.

"He's swimming," a disdainful voice reported.

"The fool."

"Don't be too hard on him. He's an imbecile."

There was a floundering in the water, and a louder splash.

"Hold him under," whispered Boris. "He'll ruin everything."

"Quiet. Stay still. There's somebody on the boat."

They looked up at the bow of the trawler. A match flared as a cigarette was lit.

"It's the Captain. Don't move."

It was the longest cigarette Vorolokov had ever smoked. Even from twenty yards they could see his face each time he drew a lungful of smoke. He seemed to be staring straight at them as they lay on the wet mattress of seaweed.

At last, the cigarette end arced down from the bow, and they heard a cabin door shut.

There was a knitting-circle noise behind Boris.

"What is it, this time?" he asked exasperated.

"Guess whose teeth," said a voice.

"Tell Igor to come up here so's I can smash his head on a rock."

There was a whisper.

"He says he's sorry, but he can't move. He says he's frozen. He's been lying in the sea for ten minutes."

A dog panted ahead of them.

"It's us, Lev."

They rose to a crouch and approached. The dog's tail thumped Lev's boot at the smell of the cook.

"The sentry's up by the gate. Sacha's talking to him."

"Good man."

They crawled along the wire till they came to the water's edge. They eased themselves in and swam along a line parallel to the latrines.

They were only just in time.

Top Sergeant Elliot Hennessey boasted he was the only coloured Irishman in the American Marines. He was born in Alabama and claimed as a great-grandfather an Irish planter who had settled there 125 years before. He was proud of his name, proud of his ancestry, but proudest of being a Marine.

A Vietnam veteran, wounded twice in action, he had already served nine years in the Marines. And he wanted to stay in the Corps.

He was a sad-faced man. He led a well-regulated life. He washed every day at the same time. He cleaned his boots every day at the same time. His life was governed by a self-imposed timetable.

By his watch it was 9 p.m. It was time for him to visit the latrine.

Hennessey liked music. His preference was for what he called Irish spirituals. But, unlike the people of his races — Negro or Irish — he had no mastery at all over his vocal chords. He was, in fact, completely tone deaf.

He pushed aside the tarpaulin door of a latrine tent, lowered his trousers and sat down. He liked this quiet part of the day. It was the only time he could sing in private.

"If you ever go across the sea to Ireland. It may be at the closing of your days. . . ." He stopped for a moment, and strained noisily.

Boris hauled himself out of the water.

"They're at it again." He beckoned his Commandos to follow. Quietly, they made their way to the shadows between the two American buildings. The moon was rising. There were no clouds.

The slaughterhouse sounds increased until the Russians found it almost unendurable.

"Must we wait? Can't we go in and rescue him?"

75

"No, Igor. Stick to the plan."

The howling stopped. The small tent shuddered, and Hennessey stepped into the moonlight, buttoning his trousers. The moon illuminated his white singlet.

He had taken only two paces when Boris's Commandos leapt. A blanket engulfed him. He was too startled to cry out. His half-buttoned trousers fell to his ankles, tripping him.

He heard a voice say close to his ear: "Be most silence. We frens."

The long blanket, wound tightly round him, stopped him from struggling. He felt his feet leave the ground, as strong arms carried him like a roll of linoleum.

"Boris, look Igor." The urgent tone made Boris stop. He realised something catastrophic was about to happen. He spun round. The American sentry was still talking to Sacha. He was lighting the Russian's cigarette. Only a few yards behind him, both arms raised, stood Igor. The moonlight glinted on the massive monkey-wrench used for opening the trawler's sea cocks.

Boris seldom moved fast. But he covered the distance between himself and Igor in almost one silent bound. With one hand he snatched the three-foot wrench. With his other arm he swung Igor off his feet and back into the shadows. He pressed him against the wall of a hut. Igor's feet trod air.

"You brainless Cossack," he seethed. "Why do you want to kill everyone?"

Boris dragged him down to the sea and pushed him ahead of him in the direction of the trawler.

The party carrying the rescued Negro kept to the water's edge till it reached the stern of the trawler and the black shadows beneath the hull.

A rope snaked down from the lifeboat davits, and was fastened round Hennessey's waist. Blackened hands tugged. His figure shot up into the air and was bundled onto the deck.

"All clear."

The Commando rescue party swarmed aboard.

In the crew's quarters, they sat Hennessey on the edge of a bunk and unwrapped him.

76

He wasn't exactly white. But certainly grey.

He squared his shoulders. "You won't get nothing outa me. 14715094 Top Sergeant Elliot M. Hennessey, US Marine Corps. That's all."

"We frens. We rescue you."

"You ain't tricking me with your psychological stuff. I'm 14715094 Top Sergeant Elliot M. Hennessey, US Marine Corps. And that sure is all."

Boris handed him a mug of vodka.

"You ain't trying to get me drugged."

"Is goot vodka," said Boris. He took a swig at the mug. It leaked down his black chin.

"If you think your minstrel dress is gonna trick me into thinking you're one of my folk, you're wrong."

"We's comrades," insisted Boris. "We rescue you from white torturers who oppress you."

"I ain't oppressed, bud, I'm American. And I don't wanna be rescued."

If the Russians had spoken perfect English, it would have taken them a long time to explain the situation. With their vague knowledge, and Vasili's dictionary it was almost impossible.

"Us mistook . . ." Boris searched through the small book. "Manoeuvre . . . rescue . . . er." He searched again. ". . . misconstruction . . . ridiculous."

What little English Boris knew was lost in his embarrassment.

"Please . . . excuse . . . we desolate." "We hear . . . scream . . . much howling. Think . . . torture . . . agony."

"Howling? Agony?" Hennessey was puzzled. "I was singing." He was furious.

Boris hunted for the translations of Russian apologies.

"Boy, are we in a mess," said Hennessey at last, as he began to make some sense of the conversation. "If I don't get back, my boys'll charge right in here and get me. An' if they see me over here being friendly, they'll think I've defected. And if you lot get caught, they'll bust you right out of the Red Navy."

"What we do?"

"I'll tell you. First you smuggle me out of here, quiet like so your officers don't know. Then you smuggle me back into our sector so's mine don't find out. And while we're doing it, you pray like you never prayed before—whoever you pray to. I'd sure hate to be the guy who starts the Third World War."

Vorolokov worked late, checking the ship's papers. It was a couple of hours before Igor reported that his cabin light had at last gone out. The Russians reversed the rescue operation. This time, however, Hennessey walked. The moon was behind clouds.

He waded round the end of the wire, then followed the barrier till he was level with them. His teeth made a disembodied grin in the darkness.

"Well, fellas, thanks for the thought, anyway."

The teeth vanished. They heard him turn and pad softly away to the tents.

Luigi Morelli was the only Marine to wear his steel helmet all the time. He wasn't nervous. He wasn't afraid. It was just that the helmet was the only method of hiding his transistor radio earplug. He wore it with the cord over the top of his ear and carefully tucked between his blue chin and helmet strap. The radio was carried in a webbing shoulder-holster under his tunic. A large boil plaster covered the short length of wire between the chin strap and his tightly buttoned collar.

Morelli was a baseball addict. Incurable and single-minded. He listened to every transmission on baseball. And in order to follow his sport, this often meant listening while he was on duty.

"Morelli," an officer would bawl. There'd be no reaction. Morelli's eyes focused on some distant object. But his attention was on the even more distant San Francisco Giants.

During the daytime, he cultivated absentmindedness. He deliberately left his flies undone, his boots untied. Sometimes he wore odd socks. Sometimes no socks at all. When he knew it was safe, he wore parts of his equipment upside down. He was a professional soldier, and knew how far to take his eccentricity.

"MO-REL-LI! Wake up!" He'd return to his post with a jolt. The look of brown eyed innocence which he practised for hours in front of his shaving mirror usually kept him out of trouble. But, in fact, it fooled nobody. Everyone knew what he was doing.

It was early evening, the dull couple of hours after dinner when the Marines sat around preparing their kit. The nightly poker school in the Mess had not yet begun. It was warm. The men sat in the open. It was seven-fifteen, and

Hennessey was cleaning his M.16. He had another twenty-five minutes before his next ritual—inspecting the guard. The guard tonight was Morelli.

Victoria lounged back against the entrance of the PX store, surrounded by her usual retinue of Marines. They were her slaves. She was not allowed to do anything for herself, or for anyone else.

Zeke, the Kentucky chef, watched her with big brother interest. He forbade her to cook.

"Ain't no need. Four extra's no difference to me."

He was her protector. It took the young Marines only a few days to find that the degree of their friendship with Victoria governed the size of their meals. If they stepped beyond Zeke's Presbyterian limits their food portions shrank. His method never failed. A man can starve for so long.

Sometimes, the men cajoled and threatened. But Zeke outranked them in several ways. He was a corporal. He was the tallest in the section. And he had the quickest temper.

Albert was choked. He knew Victoria was as eager for him as ever. She wanted to be alone with him. But in the daytime, eyes followed them everywhere. In the evening, the eyes' owners did the trailing. In the tent, there was Rhodes, Collins—and the canvas wall. Albert's sleep was ruined by nightmares.

He would find himself alone with Victoria on the plateau. They'd be naked. Passionate. Their bodies pressing together. Gently, he would ease forward . . .

Then, crash. The onrushing steel bow of a ship would claw its way up rock towards them, its rails packed with an applauding audience. He would wake up, shivering and angry.

Morelli, his carbine slung over his shoulder, strolled along the white line beside the barrier. He reached the limpet-sharp rocks at the southern side of the plateau, and turned back. He'd been on duty for an hour, and had another hour before he'd be relieved.

To him his sentry turn was less of a bore than to the other Grunts. He was only on duty physically.

80

It was a good game. The St Louis Cardinals were now two runs ahead. Lou Brock had just struck a homer. Listening needed his full concentration. Static crackled Morelli's earpiece.

For the twenty-eighth time, he passed the Russian guard and his dog. Both watched him closely. They were fascinated by this extraordinary Marine whose face was a changing kaleidoscope of emotion. Sometimes he grinned. Sometimes he scowled. His breath would whistle between his teeth. Often, he would raise a fist to the sky, and mutter. His pace changed with his expressions. When he grinned, it was springy. When he scowled, he dragged his feet. Occasionally, he skipped for a yard or two. Other times, he stopped altogether, and screwed up his face in furrowed concentration.

"Hey, Morelli, chow." Zeke stationed himself in Morelli's path, but the guard's feet, automatically reacting to an obstacle in his course, took a pace sideways and continued their somnambulant beat.

"Luigi, ya dumb Wop. Here's your ketchup sandwich. Get rid of it before the Sergeant does his round."

He thrust a drooling sandwich into Morelli's limp hand.

"Huh, thanks."

He continued to tramp along the barrier. Red beetles of ketchup followed him as they dribbled from his sandwich.

The game was at its climax.

The Russian guard and the dog watched him approaching. The dog's nose twitched. Morelli reached the point of his patrol when he was nearest to them. They were separated now only by the wire barrier itself. The dog suddenly darted into the barrier, dragging its handler against the sharp points. He let go the lead. Unimpeded, the dog accelerated through the remaining coils of wire and hit Morelli in the small of the back. The dog was heavy. The impact jerked Morelli's transistor earpiece out, and drove him face down into the rock.

He felt a wet mouth close over his hand. He jerked his arm away. Then he remembered his training and lay still. He could feel the weight of the dog on his rump.

He heard shouts all round him. The Russian was trying to recall his dog. Morelli's friends were scrambling to help

81

him. He heard the rattle of a carbine bolt. The weight suddenly left him.

He was helped to his feet. The dog was loping towards the stern of the trawler. The Soviet guard appeared to be apologising. A stream of Russian came from him. But his voice was lost in furious shouts from the American Marines.

Morelli examined himself. He was unhurt, but winded and shaken.

Second-Lieutenant Alton C. Ellsmore strode into the pack of Marines and questioned him.

"Did you tease the dog, Morelli?"

"Didn't even see it, sir."

"Take twenty," said Ellsmore. "Get yourself a coffee. By the way, is your hearing aid okay?"

"Hearing aid, sir?"

"This must be the dog's then." The subultern smirked, and tugged the earpiece with its short wire from Morelli's collar. He tossed it over the wire into the Russian sector.

"And fasten your flies."

The young Lieutenant was unpopular. He enjoyed his new authority. The Island was his first taste of action. He stood at the barrier and in the military Russian he had learned at academy he demanded to see the senior Soviet officer. Vorolokov was called from the Mess table. He was apologetic. He assured Ellsmore it would not happen again. The dog would be kept further back from the wire in future.

There was a smug look on the Lieutenant's face as he turned away from the frontier and stalked over to his major's tent to report his success. The Marines watched him go. "Next thing we know, he'll be walking on the water," said Morelli.

The Russians were mystified by their dog's attack. Rasputin was evil only in name. Despite his appearance, he was not a guard dog. He was the ship's pet. He loved everyone. Even birds took his mashed food unpunished. The attack was quite out of character. But the Americans didn't know this. They'd often heard growls and the rough, rather high-pitched barks as it was led on patrol along the wire. Only the Russians knew it was Lev making the appropriate dog noises, taking his cue from the jaw movements of his silent companion. For Rasputin was a mute.

The incident did nothing to relieve the tension between the two sectors.

Morelli was on guard duty again the next evening. This time, he was bored. The transistor was too big to fit inside his helmet. He knew he couldn't play it at full volume under his tunic: he just wouldn't get away with that. Instead, he passed the time thinking of effective ways of getting his revenge on Ellsmore, the man who put him in this predicament. He even thought of sneaking into the Soviet sector to find his earpiece, but he couldn't see it from his side of the barrier. It must have fallen into a crevice.

Zeke brought him his usual tomato ketchup sandwich. Once more Morelli patrolled the wire.

He was standing twenty yards from the dog, and heard it snuffle. Again, it pulled towards the wire. This time, prepared, Morelli dropped his sandwich, and unslung his carbine. Then he looked. The dog no longer watched him. Its eyes were on the sandwich. It still strained at its leash.

The Russian guard, pulling back against the weight, half-smiled at Morelli and nodded at the sandwich. Morelli looked at the snuffling dog, then at the sandwich. He remembered the wet mouth on the hand which had held the uneaten snack the night before.

"So that's it," he thought, "They're not feeding him enough."

He grinned at the Russian, and kicked the sandwich towards Rasputin.

The guard slackened the chain and let the dog lead him towards the wire. It pushed between the barbed strands, grabbed the pink bread, and wriggled itself out backwards. The sandwich was gone in two gulps. The dog sat on its haunches and looked at Morelli. Then it begged.

The guard pulled the dog back onto its feet, smiled again at the Marine and put a finger to his lips.

Morelli hitched his carbine back onto his shoulder and resumed his patrol. As he walked, a plan started to form in his mind. He put it into action when his second spell of duty began at midnight. The camp was asleep. Morelli crept away from his post by the wire and disappeared into the unoccupied Mess. He emerged with a large bulge in the front of his tunic.

He picked a cautious route through the rocks to the Lieutenant's tent, listened, then crawled noiselessly inside.

He reappeared almost immediately, and backed, crouching, to the wire, squeezing a plastic bottle onto the ground as he went. He reached into the wire and squirted the remainder of the bottle onto the foot of the barrier. The puddle glistened in the moonlight. Morelli walked quickly away from the wire, and resumed his watch from a rocky seat by the American arc-lamps on the edge of the plateau.

The Russian guard walking the dog around the perimeter of the Soviet sector reached the wire. Morelli could hear it sniffing.

The dog reached the barrier near Morelli's puddle and sat down. The guard gave its leash a tug. The dog stiffened its front legs and with a bunching of his muscles tore the chain out of the Russian's hands. It charged the wire barrier and, stopping only briefly at the puddle, it vacuum-cleaned its way along the juicy trail Morelli had laid. It loped, sniffing, licking and slobbering, over the plateau. It circled Rhodes's orange office, then dived into the end pup tent.

From inside came affectionate noises. Then a soft, slurping, sounding like wet kisses. There was a suppressed moan, then a terrified scream. The thirty-six inch high tent rose from the ground as the six-foot Lieutenant surged to his feet inside it. The tent shuddered, and keeled over onto the neighbouring tent. There was another, louder, scream. Muffled panting and shouts filtered through the struggling heap of canvas.

"Save me. I'm being savaged."

Lights flashed as Marines crawled out of the tents. The camp woke in confusion.

Corrigan's voice rose above the uproar.

"Switch on the arc-lamps."

Morelli threw the switch.

Half the tent-line looked hurricane-wrecked. Three of the canvas shelters on the western side of the square were collapsed. The occupants of two had managed to free themselves. The third tent screamed, shook and shuddered. Corrigan strode over, grabbed the edge of the canvas, and peeled it off.

Ace Ellsmore lay writhing on his sleeping bag. He seemed

to be covered with blood. He was holding the guard dog away by its collar. It was trying to get at him.

Corrigan snatched a carbine from the nearest Marine, and raised the butt to smash down on the dog. Then he noticed the alsatian was not snarling, but was trying to lick the Lieutenant.

The Major sniffed, frowned, then sniffed again. The animal glanced at him, pulled itself backwards out of Ace's grip, rolled onto its back, and feebly paddled its feet in the air.

Corrigan slowly lowered the gun. Sergeant Hennessey bent over and rubbed the dog's stomach. Its eyes rolled.

He turned the dog onto its feet. It cavorted and gambolled, its tail fanning.

"Rasputin. Rasputin."

From the other side of the barrier came Lev's desperate voice.

The dog's ears flicked. But it ignored the command. It just sat back on its haunches and looked stupidly at Corrigan.

"I'm dying," groaned the Lieutenant. He sat up. His face, hands, pyjamas and sleeping bag were stained. "My God, I've been eaten. Look at my blood. Get the plasma."

Corrigan knelt beside him. "You smell like a hamburger," he said.

He wiped his hand across the red stains on the fawn silk pyjamas, and touched his fingers to his tongue.

"How long you been bleeding ketchup, son?"

There was a yowl of laughter from the delighted Marines, enjoying the Lieutenant's sticky discomfort.

Morelli sucked his chin strap and tried to look more innocent than usual. Again, it didn't fool anyone.

The Kentucky cook staggered over to him, hung a lean arm round Morelli's shoulder and sagged at the knees as he tried to speak through convulsed gasps.

"Man, oh man. You sure got that one licked for us. . . . Tomorrow, ah'm going to cook you the biggest steak in . . . the world . . . Kayntuck style . . . with ketchup."

Corrigan was having a hard time playing it straight-faced. He turned so his expression was hidden in the shadows.

"Get down to the sea, son, and get washed," he growled. "And come and speak to me in the morning. You and I are going to discuss the facts of life." He turned to Hennessey. "Get this camp straight, Sergeant. And find out who set this up."

He strode off towards his tent. As he passed Morelli, he spoke out of the corner of his mouth. "Don't push your luck, bootneck."

"Who, me, sir?"

"Yes, you with the ketchup on your boots."

Morelli walked a lonely night watch. He didn't mind. He was listening to a game between the Detroit Tigers and the Cleveland Indians through his new earpiece. It fitted into his ear even more comfortably than his old one. He'd found it in a folded paper, taped to his helmet. The paper, in Ellsmore's handwriting, read: "The hatchet is buried—okay?"

9 Rasputin now had dual nationality. As the days passed, he got fatter. He'd learnt the meal timetable on both sides of the wire. Now that his true harmlessness was known, he was no longer regarded as a watchdog. He had the freedom of the Island.

His day began with a biscuit with Vorolokov, then breakfast with the Russian crew. This was followed by ketchup and cornflakes with Morelli in the American sector. Mid-morning would find him back on the trawler where he knew Boris would be clearing the galley scraps. An hour later, he would help Zeke sort the American cookhouse garbage.

This usually took him until lunch began on the *Dmitri Kirov*. He would sleep for an hour in the sun on the rocks below the trawler, and would wake refreshed and hungry for the titbits now available in the American Mess.

His afternoon was divided between the two cooks, Zeke and Boris. He was a persuasive beggar. By six in the evening, he was so crammed, he had little room for the Russian evening meal. Supper with the Americans was an effort. His only exercise was his walk from one meal to another.

The Americans were now enjoying the Island. It was obvious they'd have no trouble from the Russian seamen. The Marines knew the Russians' crash-damaged equipment was still inoperative, and would remain unworkable until the autumn. The Americans' jamming gear wouldn't reach them for several weeks. Corrigan's orders were to hold the Island and establish a base. In the meantime discipline was slightly relaxed. Parades and arms-drills were minimal. There were still guard duties, but the men carried batons now instead of rifles.

87

Lieutenant Ace Ellsmore was studying to become human. It was taking him time, but he was learning its advantages. He had a feeling now that if he were wounded in battle, his men would actually rush to rescue him. Before, he felt, they might not have been so eager.

"Get to know them," Major Corrigan told him. "These are Grunts. Got tradition since 1775. Treat 'em right and they'll follow you anywhere. And respect them. Most were in action when you were at High School."

The only tension, now, came from the loudspeaker which Major Corrigan set up near the wire. It wasn't his idea, and it annoyed him as much as it deafened the Russians. For an hour every morning and afternoon, it blared out tape-recorded propaganda in 'Russian'. None of the Marines could understand a word. It was too fast, Ellsmore claimed, even for him.

To the Russians, the loudspeaker was just noise. Someone back on the U.S. Fleet had boobed. The tapes were in Albanian.

The Russians countered by bolting a speaker on the bow of the trawler. This was switched on at the same time as the U.S. speaker. To the Americans, the Russians' broadcast was even more incomprehensible. It was tuned into the British Broadcasting Corporation's cricket commentaries.

For an hour in the morning, and an hour in the evening, everyone had headaches.

Corrigan's men had so much time on their hands that every item of their equipment was kept in text-book order. Footdrill was out of the question: the men couldn't march over the rough rocks. Corrigan thought of ways of keeping his men occupied. He would have followed the British army tradition of painting white everything that didn't move. But the cormorants and seagull had done this for him.

He introduced competitions to keep the men busy. He arranged a shooting match. The men unenthusiastically took part. They knew that Zeke would win. He tried unarmed combat. The men were just as disinterested. There wasn't much fun in being smashed against the rocks by Joe Suki, the Navy judo champion.

Swimming was the most popular contest. Corrigan allowed Victoria and Albert to compete. The Marines usually let her win, but there was always a scramble for second place, as the man got a consolation kiss. Albert, a good swimmer, invariably found himself hemmed in by three or four water-polo playing Grunts. He never finished higher than fourth.

In the Russian sector Vorolokov found no problem keeping his seamen occupied. All they wanted to do was to fish. The Russian Navy didn't provide fishing gear because it never expected the *Dmitri Kirov* to be used for that purpose. So the men made their own. They forged hooks and filched nylon lines from aerial kites and weather balloons. Bronze brazing rods were converted into lobster pots, which they laid off the rocks. Sacha's net was now finished.

Igor watched the basking sharks, finning through the mackerel shoals that drifted near the Island. He shaped a jemmy into a fierce harpoon head, and set it into the haft of a broken oar. The weapon was eight feet long. The detachable head was spliced to a hundred feet of signal halyard. He practised for hours, throwing it at a floating barrel. He never got the opportunity to use it on a shark— they seemed to be psychic, and stayed away.

At first, Ushakov, the scientist, didn't fish. He swam. He sunbathed. And played endless games of chess against colleagues on the Soviet fleet far out at sea. The messages from the Island to these ships gave American Intelligence hours of worry. At first, they didn't know whether the chess moves were genuine or coded signals. Eventually, they solved the problem by setting up their own chessboard and paralleling the moves. The American Intelligence men became enthused with the chessboard duels.

"Good God, no!" One of them groaned. "He's committing hara-kiri. He should have kept his queen back, and attacked with the knight." He had money on the losing player. A sweepstake was run on the Soviet games, and more American money was gambled on the outcome than Russian.

The Marine General on the Sixth Fleet ordered over the radio-telephone: "No more radio, Red Member. Keep to complete silence, except in emergencies. Dropping you carrier pigeons from Germany for future contact. Don't call us, we'll call you."

89

Corrigan thumbed the switch urgently, "What about Red Member's Indep . . ." He was interrupted.

"Think Mamma forgot her favourite baby? We're dropping little Linus his special Independence Day rations at the same time. Out."

July 4th was also Vorolokov's birthday. He would be forty-nine. His crew planned a celebration, a fish barbecue. For days they had been storing lobsters in a wire keep, set below the water level near the trawler's stern. Tanya sewed together the white sweater she had knitted him.

It was July 2nd. Albert and Victoria had been on the Island for three weeks. Albert was beginning to feel that the name of the Island should have been Alcatraz. They weren't allowed off it. They couldn't even visit neighbouring islands. Albert worried about the Biograph. Corrigan had let him cable Manny for extended leave. He knew the manager would look after the old age pensioners, and the pensioners after the mice, but who would look after Manny? That's what bothered him.

He hadn't imagined that being a millionaire could be so limiting.

"Don't worry," Collins told him. "Think of the interest your money's earning in the bank."

"I've already got my interests, here," said Albert, thinking of Victoria. "But I can't get my hands on that either," he added quietly.

Collins liked draughts. At home he played them in the pub every evening. On the Island, he played checkers with Zeke. Unlike Albert, he was enjoying his enforced rest. He certainly didn't miss his wife's continual stews. Zeke's cooking was better.

Rhodes had cause to worry. His gin stock was disturbingly low. The radio ban and their quarantine meant no relief supplies. He was rationing himself to half-tumblers, and even considered stretching it out with the help of the Americans' Coca-Cola. But he decided to postpone this emergency.

His band of grey hair needed cutting. It now sprouted from the side of his head like the tattered brim of a straw hat. The bedraggled red wig now rested on it with less ease than before.

Victoria bubbled. She owned a male harem, fifteen tough, bronzed sea-soldiers, who wooed her continuously. She was a goddess, with a millionaire in tow.

"Gee, honey, we'll soon be alone," she told Albert when he complained. "I dig you the most."

But this only made matters worse. Her growing American vocabulary only reinforced his protests that she was seeing too much of the Marines.

An aircraft droned nearer. It glinted in the sunlight as it homed on the Island. It circled them. A smoking orange parachute flare dropped beneath it and swung slowly towards them.

"Supplies," shouted the American sentry.

"Launch the dinghy." Corrigan called the men. "Make it quick. We may lose something in the sea."

The plane made a run upwind, diagonally across the Island. The pilot narrowly avoided violating Soviet air space. The Russians on the deck of the trawler stood, faces upwards. They saw three bundles drop. White parachutes umbrellaed open, and drifted towards the Island.

It was a good drop. The Island was a small target, the American sector even smaller. The bundles splashed into the sea, thirty feet off shore, and were collected almost immediately by the waiting Marines.

The aircraft made a second run. The door between the twin fuselages opened. It gave birth ...

"Holy cow," said Ace Ellsmore. "Just what we needed—a jeep."

Clusters of parachutes burst open above each end of the falling vehicle.

"A dollar gets you five it lands on the Mess," offered Clancy Paradise.

"I'll take that. I'll stake ten, said Corrigan.

Two final bundles were thrown from the aircraft.

"They'll never make the Island," said a voice.

The jeep was clearly falling towards the sea.

"Shell out," said Corrigan to Paradise.

A cell of wind caught the jeep. It pendulumed towards the men.

"TIM-BERRR," shouted Corrigan.

The load was now aiming at the flagpole. It zapped it at

an angle of forty-five degrees. There was a splintering. The top of the flagpole jack-knifed. The flag was snatched by the jeep and carried away.

The spinning vehicle just cleared the barbed wire barrier and the ducked heads of the Soviet guards, and slewed to a halt on the flat ground in front of the trawler. The parachutes died, sinking to the rocks. The Stars and Stripes looked back at the Americans from its new home in the Soviet sector.

"Thanks for nothing," Morelli shouted at the retreating aircraft.

"What happened to the rest of the crap?" someone asked.

There was silence, as eyes scanned the sea and the surrounding rocks.

"That plane musta been flown by a Russian—look!"

They looked. A plastic drum was hanging by its parachute from the stern radio mast of the *Dmitri Kirov*. It was unnoticed by the Russians, who were more interested in the jeep. They stood around it in a group.

The radio operator called Corrigan over. He picked up the headset. "Have you received the supplies?" asked a voice.

"The three first bundles. The jeep's gone to the Russians. And the black drum. What was in it?"

"Your turkeys. The pigeons were in a crate."

"Well, there's no sign of them," said Corrigan.

"Tough," said the voice. "Out."

Zeke appeared through the doorway of the radio tent.

"They ain't sent mah turkeys, sir," he said.

"They have," replied Corrigan. "That's them hanging on the trawler."

A voice called from outside. "Major, a Russian to see you, sir."

Corrigan went out, and walked over to the wire where the scientist, Ushakov, was standing.

"Is this yours?" he grinned, handing Corrigan the carefully folded Stars and Stripes.

Corrigan took it. "What about the jeep?" he asked.

"Uhh!" said Ushakov. "What jeep?"

"That one." The major pointed.

The scientist grinned again. "If one of your men drove the

jeep into our territory we must have issued him a permit. And we don't have any permits to issue."

"It dropped in by parachute, you dumb Ruskie."

"Then it has violated Soviet airspace, and is forfeit," he said firmly. He bowed to the Major, turned and walked back.

Damn the jeep. The Russians were welcome to it. There was nowhere to drive it, anyway. But, for Corrigan's men, Independence Day wasn't the same without turkeys. Even in the front line, they'd never before missed their supply.

"Turkeys are history in my outfit," Corrigan would tell his new recruits. "We get 'em because men died. Men died so's you'd be here to eat turkeys. No other unit in the Corps gets turkey on Independence Day. We do."

This introductory speech would be followed by a capsuled account of the Corps' battle honours, from 1775 until the present day. The turkeys were an award to Corrigan's unit for heroism in Korea. "The Gooks came at us in hundreds on Independence Day." Corrigan would shut his eyes, remembering the mud and blood of the war. "There were sixteen of us. We held 'em off for five days. Afterwards, there were only eight of us left. All wounded. They counted three hundred and sixty dead Gooks in front of us. The General said it looked like we'd had a turkey shoot. Then he gave us medals. And, for all time, turkey for the men of this unit on Independence Day. Whenever you eat turkey in future, think of the dead Grunts and the honours of the U.S. Marine Corps."

"Ah got the cranberry sauce and apple sauce orl ready," grumbled Zeke. "It's sure a shame to waste it. Anybody fancy them black birds asittin' on that rock?" He pointed at the two ragged cormorants on their usual outcrop. There were no takers. The birds smelt bad enough alive. Only the Lord knew what they would be like dead.

"How much if I get the turkeys?" asked Joe Suki.

"No chance," said Zeke.

"Sure, I can," said Joe.

"I'll give a five spot," said Morelli.

"Me, too."

The other Marines agreed.

93

"I don't want to know," said the Major. "But I'll chip in another five if I get turkey on July 4th."

"Leave it to me, kids." Suki's slight Oriental features beamed. He flexed his massive shoulders. His deltoids taughtened. "We'll be defrosting those turkeys tonight. Help me dress."

Suki was a Filipino, one of the Marines' Beach Reconnaissance Team—a frogman. He was hustled into the Mess. The men collected his gear. Suki stripped, and rubbed himself with talcum, then pulled himself into his neoprene tights. He struggled into the jacket, and eased on the socks. He zipped himself up, and pushed his head into the black hood. Then he strapped a long knife on his calf. Hands lifted compressed-air bottles onto his back. A Marine handed him his weight belt. Suki clipped it round his waist. With a familiar shrug, he swung the air tubes over his head. "Turn me on," he said. A hand unscrewed the valve.

He reached under his armpit and grabbed the gauge swinging on a short length of hose. He checked the bottle pressure, then sucked a lungful of air through his mouthpiece.

Like a surgeon asking for his operating instruments, Suki said:

"Gloves, mask, fins."

"It's all clear. The Russians are still going over the jeep," said Clancy Paradise.

They crowded Suki out of the Mess, and down to the shore.

Corrigan saw them, but immediately turned away on some make-believe mission.

"Best of luck, Suki," said Ace Ellsmore, working hard on his new cameraderie.

"Thank *you*, sir," said the surprised Filipino.

He stepped into the water, rubbed spit onto the glass visor of his mask and adjusted it over his face. Then he pulled on his gloves and fins. He floated out backwards, pushing the mouthpiece between his teeth.

Even over the ten yards that separated them, they could hear the hiss of his breathing. He turned over and slid from sight. They watched the trail of bubbles as he headed for deeper water, and the Russian sector . . .

"He's a brave kid," said the Lieutenant who was eight years younger than Suki.

Boris the Russian cook had barely given the jeep a glance. To him it was just a hunk of dull machinery. It wasn't as interesting as his new bait. He was trying the limpets he'd chiselled off the rocks. They were highly successful. At the moment, he had a large conger eel fighting in a sack at his feet. He was holding the strong line delicately in his big hands.

The bite, when it came, whipped the cord through his fingers. It cut deep into the flesh. This was a sea monster.

"Igor," shouted Boris. "Come quick."

The young Cossack leapt from rock to rock to the cook's side.

"Pull," shouted Boris. Igor grabbed the line and put a turn round his wrist. He was almost dragged into the water.

"Help me play it, you fool. It'll break the line."

The two men hauled on the fish. It dragged yards of line into the water, but they gradually drew it back. It surged forward again.

"Easy," coaxed Boris.

"My harpoon," panted Igor.

"Get it—fast."

The monster fish was now only a few yards out in the thick seaweed.

Igor ran up the rocks. "We've got a shark," he shouted. "My harpoon."

It was dropped to him from the trawler. The fishermen ran back with him to Boris. Many hands grabbed the line from the panting cook. His palms were slashed and bleeding where the line had burnt deep furrows through them. The fishermen could just make out the glint of the fish as it threshed in the leathery kelp.

Igor drew back his arm and launched his harpoon. It ricocheted off with a clang. The fish stood up on two feet and charged at the Russians. Boris fell backwards into the water.

The black sea monster seized Igor and threw him after his harpoon.

"Keeaiy . . ." it screamed, charging the other stupefied Russians. It felled Sacha with one quick chop.

95

"Frogman," Boris cried belatedly as the figure shook the air bottles from its shoulders, and kicked off its fins. "Hold him."

Igor splashed out of the sea, and threw himself at the figure. It side-stepped, and accelerated Igor on his way with a deft push. Igor cannoned into a rock, spun, recovered, and charged again. A foot tripped him. A hip lifted him into the air. He found himself back in the sea.

Suki stood, his feet balanced lightly on a rock, picking the Russians off as they attacked him. He was calm and enjoying himself. He might have been back on the dojo mats, instructing the Navy judo team.

He called out the names of the throws as he disposed of his attackers. "Ashi-guruma!" A Russian cartwheeled backwards.

"Kata-seoi!" He grabbed a Russian by the arm and spun him high over his shoulder.

"Tomoe-nage!" He dropped backwards, put his foot into Lev's stomach and catapulted him over his head into the shallows.

He had just executed a spectacular Utsui-goshi on Vasili, dropping him heavily on his back on the rocks, when Ushakov stepped up with a sub-machinegun. Reluctantly, Suki put up his arms. The Russian prodded his captive with the barrel. It was painful—for Ushakov. For Suki used one of the defences unarmed Samurai warriors developed, Aikido. He swept his left arm down in an arc, trapped Ushakov's left hand against the front grip of the machine-gun, lifted the muzzle and stepped underneath. Ushakov had time to become interested in the technique even before he left the ground. He was surprised to find that he was in the air long enough to get a clear upside-down picture of Igor crashing the shaft of the harpoon onto the frogman's head.

Ushakov and Suki recovered consciousness at the same time. They were both lying on the deck of the trawler where they had been carried by the bruised Russian seamen. Suki tried to sit up, and almost impaled himself on the point of the harpoon held close to his chest by Igor. There was a wild, excited look in the young Cossack's eyes. Suki decided to lie still.

The bearded Russian officer saw Suki move, and came over. At his side stood the young dark-haired woman whom Suki had often seen from the other side of the wire. She was cradling the sub-machinegun in her arms.

"This is spying," said the officer. "For this you can be shot. You have invaded our territory. You have injured my men. Twice in one day your people have violated our land. This is great provocation."

Suki swallowed. He decided the most sensible course of action would be to tell the Russians the truth.

"I came for our turkeys." Even to him the excuse sounded unreal.

The frown didn't leave Vorolokov's face.

"What stupid story is this?"

"Our turkeys landed on your ship, on the stern radio mast." He pointed.

The officer turned, looked, and saw nothing.

"Can I sit up?" asked Suki.

"Stand up. If you try to escape we will shoot."

Suki lumbered to his feet and looked towards the stern. The turkeys weren't visible from the deck. He realised that he would have to convince Vorolokov quickly.

"Can I show you?" he asked. He hoped they were still there.

"No." Vorolokov spat a command at one of the seamen in Russian. The man clambered over the side of the ship, dropped down the ladder and walked away. He looked up to the stern of the trawler. "Da," he shouted.

Vorolokov spoke again in Russian. Two other seamen disappeared towards the rear of the ship.

Suki was assessing the size of the bump on the back of his head. It seemed to fill his entire palm. He was wondering how he was going to remove his close-fitting diving hood, when the two seamen returned, carrying the heavy black container.

They lowered it carefully to the deck in front of their officer.

"Open it," he said. "No. You open it." He pointed at Suki.

The Russians stepped back. Suki bent over the plastic drum.

"Remember the gun. Please move slowly."

97

With exaggerated care, Suki unlatched the fasteners. The insulated lid came off smoothly. He laid it on the deck. Small blocks of ice shattered as they tumbled out.

"Enough," said Vorolokov. He said something else in Russian.

A thickset, unshaven man, with bandages on both hands and still-wet hair, stepped to the container. Suki recognised him as his first victim, and deliberately avoided his eyes.

Boris painfully brushed aside the ice splinters with the sides of his hands and lifted out a polythene package. Five similar parcels followed it, making a neat line on the deck.

He unwrapped one. His eyes glistened with professional interest as he examined the bird. It was huge. To him it was more exciting than any woman. He licked his lips. Its breast was white, full and voluptuous. Its legs shapely, with not too much sinew. Its unblemished back was smooth and delicately proportioned. Enraptured, he caressed it.

He was dragged from his culinary eroticism by a command. "Put your hand inside," said Vorolokov. "Make sure it's empty."

Boris stuffed his fat hand through the poulterer's opening. "There's something there," he said. "It's hard."

"Aaahhhh," said Vorolokov. "Get it out. Take care."

Boris gingerly closed his fingers over the package inside, and tried to withdraw his hand. It was impossible. The frozen narrow opening gripped his clenched fist. He pulled. Nothing happened. Red-faced, he wedged the turkey under his arm and tugged with his other hand. It still refused to move.

"I can't get my hand out," he said simply.

"You're worse than an ape." Vorolokov was impatient. "Let go of the thing inside. We'll shake it out."

Boris did as he was told. The turkey dropped to the deck with a thump. The package fell out. A transparent envelope of frozen giblets skated to Vorolokov's feet.

They searched the remaining five turkeys. Vorolokov turned to Suki. "You Americans have no food?"

"Sure we've got food."

"Then why you risk your life to get this birds?"

Suki decided that it would be more tactful to avoid the whole truth about the turkey ritual.

98

"It's Independence Day food," he said.

"Independence Day?"

"Uhuh." He thought quickly. "Like your May Day. It's the day we got our freedom. It's the day after tomorrow."

"The day after tomorrow is mine birthday." The Russian officer smiled. "You are very foolish man. But very strong. You fight my whole crew for six birds. They must be much importance to you."

Suki felt the pendulum swing in his favour, and kept quiet.

"I have never eaten such gross turkey," grinned Vorolokov. "I give you your freedom for two birds. But don't being so stupid again."

Suki nodded agreement. He bundled four turkeys and the giblet packets into the container, clamped the lid back on, and hoisted the drum easily onto his shoulder. He was in a hurry. He didn't want the Russian to change his mind.

"I'll send you some cranberry sauce," he said.

His air bottles and diving gear were lying on the rocks at the bottom of the rope ladder. He balanced the equipment on the other shoulder, grinned at the row of heads watching him from the rail of the trawler, and swaggered towards the barrier.

The guard saw him, and pulled open the gate. Suki cheerfully nodded to him. And walked jauntily through, whistling Yankie Doodle.

On the American side, he was immediately surrounded by cheering Grunts.

"We were just goin' to share out your gear."

"We thought you were a gonner."

"Whatjado?"

"Howja do it?"

Suki lowered his air bottles to the ground. Then he handed the big black drum to Zeke. "You guys owe me eighty dollars," he said.

"This is the White House," said the voice.

"I'm glad you rang," said the P.M. "I want some advice."

"Sure." There was an unguarded note of surprise.

"What do you do with a droopy cactus?"

There was the sound of slow breathing over the Hot Line.

99

"What happened to it?" The words were clipped with fatherly enunciation.

"It got shaved."

"Shaved?" There was silence. "No wonder it's sagging, it's spineless," the voice chortled at its own joke. "Try propping it up with a politician. Now, about the Island . . ."

The P.M. interrupted. "But my cactus . . ."

The Texan voice stopped him. "Don't worry, I'll send you another. Now, about the Island . . ."

10

"Steaming Moses, this place is too damned hot." Hennessey, the coloured Top Sergeant, rolled his dark-brown body over in the sun.

"How's my tan goin'?"

"Fine, Sarge. You're gettin' to look more like a negro every day," laughed Suki. "Soon they won't know you're Irish."

He wriggled out of the way as Hennessey threw a half-empty Coca-Cola tin at his head.

"You slit-eyed yellow cannibal. The only white blood you got is the missionaries you ate."

Suki dived onto Hennessey's back, wrapped his thick arms round his chest, heaved him into the air and ran with him into the sea. "I'll wash you whiter than white, old buddy."

They collapsed laughing and struggling into a splutter of foam.

They turned onto their backs, and kicked their way into deeper water. They raced for almost three hundred yards.

"Hey, boy, dig that little ol' pebble we're livin' on."

They stopped and trod water. The Island was barely visible over the gentle Atlantic swell. The trawler seemed to be floating. Only the top of the orange tent and the repaired flag-mast were visible.

"Awful small place to have a war," said Suki.

"Ain't gonna be no war, kid. Them Ruskies aren't lookin' for trouble. They're not soldiers."

Hennessey's leg touched trailing seaweed. It triggered off an uncomfortable thought. "Are the sharks round here maneaters?"

"If they are, you're quite safe. It's the bull seals you want to worry about. With your suntan they'll think you're a sea

101

cow—they'll rape you. Anyway, I got my pocketknife in my shorts."

"Pocketknife ain't goin' to stop no shark."

"Don't aim to stop no shark," said Suki. "If he comes close, I'll just reach out and give your arm a nick. And when he goes for your blood, I'll just quietly swim off."

"Thanks, pal. Who needs Commies when they've friends like you?"

They swam back towards the rocks and lay floating in the shallows.

"Goin' to be a quiet time," said Hennessey. "Not a bottle of hooch between us. The Limey's got a bottle, but he don't wave it around none."

"Remember last year?" asked Suki, flicking a small black shellfish off a rock. "That stinking night in Naples. How come I always carry you home? And that cop with the sword you stole. He didn't go that Paul Revere stuff when you bent it for him. Cost us a month's pay. That was a son-of-a-bitch, and this sure is going to be, too."

"Hey, everybody, look!" Clancy Paradise stared down at them from the rocks. "There's a couple of funny coloured fish down here. The yellow one's eatin' winkles. Hey, fellas, what's yellow and eats winkles?"

There was an immediate chorus of reply. "Syphilis," shouted half a dozen voices. There were shrieks of laughter.

"Let's play ball," called Morelli. He slung the big softball to the bikini-clad Victoria. She caught it, half turned towards Albert and threw it. It missed him by five yards and was caught by Rasputin—on the other side of the wire. He tried eating it, ignoring Morelli's calls. It was retrieved after a tug-o'-war by Lev, who tossed it back to the girl.

Corrigan raised an eyebrow. This was the first open gesture of friendliness that he had seen coming from the Russians. He elbowed himself up from the rock where he'd been lying, and strolled over to the wire. He dragged a packet of Lucky Strike from his breast pocket, and offered one to Lev. The Russian seaman hesitated, then took one. Corrigan reached over the barrier and gave him a light.

"Hot," said Corrigan.

"Da," said Lev.

"Corrigan," said Corrigan, pointing at himself.

"Russian," said Lev.

"American," said Corrigan, again pointing at himself.

"Lev," said the Russian.

"Alsatian," said Corrigan, waving his hand at Rasputin.

"Russian," said Lev.

"Big," said Corrigan, drawing his hand from knee height to waist level.

"Gross," said the Russian, extending his arms sideways.

Corrigan found himself trapped in a one-word conversation. Lev was friendly but knew little English. The Marine Major felt he might offend the Russian if he ended the conversation too quickly.

He pointed at Lev. "Sailor," he said.

Lev shook his head. "Fishman."

He pointed at Corrigan. "Soldier."

This time the Major shook his head. "Marine."

Lev's eyes brightened. "Ah, sailor."

Corrigan mentally winced.

"No," he said. "Half sailor, half soldier."

"Ah," said Lev again. He laughed. He searched for a moment for the right word. "Mermaid?" he asked.

Corrigan laughed. "Kinda."

He was rescued by Victoria.

"Catch," she shouted. This time she threw the ball deliberately to the Russian, who caught it deftly. His rifle sling slid from his shoulder into the crook of his arm. He propped the weapon against a rock.

"Oi."

Lev looked over his shoulder. Igor was standing twenty yards away, cupping his hands above his head. He caught Lev's throw, and hurled the ball high over the wire. Morelli ran back several paces to catch it. He launched it even higher into the Russian sector. This time Mishca leapt forward to catch it. The softball soared into the American sector. Corrigan caught it, and threw it towards the trawler.

The teams grew. Soon, almost all the off-duty fishermen and Marines were playing. The GIs picked up the Russians' first names and yelled them as they threw them the ball. The Russians shouted back—the Americans' surnames.

103

The men were sweating. They shed clothing as they dashed about.

"Eee, Ennessee," Igor called to the coloured top-sergeant. The Cossack lobbed a large plastic marker buoy out into the sea, and ran after it. The half-dressed teams from both sides of the wire followed him. The men raced for the round orange float as it bobbed on the waves. The noisy ball game now continued in the water. It was an undisciplined water-polo match. There were no sides. The current carried the men down past the trawler. They played their way back to the shallows of the American sector.

The invisible demarcation line separating the territorial waters was forgotten. But when they staggered ashore, they instinctively splashed to their own sides of the barrier. The men relaxed in a chattering group on the rocky beach, separated only by the barbed wire. Victoria, pretending she didn't know her wet bikini was almost transparent, sat among them. Suki raided the Coca-Cola store, and came back with an armful of chilled cans. He passed them round. The cans popped and hissed as the Russians and Americans opened them. The confrontation was over.

The Soviet fishermen had been collecting driftwood for a few days, and it now stood in a pyramid a few yards in front of the trawler's bow. It caused speculation among the Americans.

Now they watched as long scrubbed tables and benches were passed down from the trawler and set up in a horseshoe around the piled driftwood.

"Igor, wacha doin'?" asked Hennessey.

Igor swung himself into a hand-balance on the back of a chair, and replied from upside down: "We make feast this night. Captain, he born day."

"Barbecue?"

"Da, lobster-fish and birds. Much vodka."

Hennessey glanced at Suki. The big Filipino licked his lips. "Much vodka?"

"Very much vodka. Very much singing."

"We're having a party tonight, too," said Suki. "Very much Coca-Cola."

Igor cartwheeled to his feet, holding the chair above his head. He looked surprised. "You no drink?"

"Sure, we like drinking. But we come from a dry ship."

Igor was puzzled.

Suki explained: "No drinks supplied."

Igor nodded sympathetically. "Maybe that why you sing bad." He pointed at Hennessey.

"Your reputation's gettin' international, Sarge."

By early evening the Russian fire was lit. The Americans watched the tables being laid, and the Russian cook bullying his helpers.

As the flames died down, and the fire became a glowing bed of charcoal, the smell of cooking and spiced sauces reached the American camp.

"Chow," shouted Zeke. The Americans sat in their Mess, awaiting their turkey. At the head of the table sat Corrigan. At the other end, in a small group, the Britons. The Kentucky cook traditionally served this special meal. He'd worked hard all day. It was perfect. Victoria, with one of Zeke's huge aprons reaching to her ankles, helped him to wait at table.

Rhodes, his wig neatly brushed, watched the Americans quietly stirring the meal with their forks. It was broody and thoughtful, not the lively celebration he'd expected.

"Say, skipper. Remember two years ago in Tokyo?" asked Morelli.

"Uhuh, weren't you a sergeant, then?" replied Corrigan.

There was laughter. They all remembered how Morelli lost his stripes.

"I still reckon it was a bath house," he said indignantly. "I was framed."

"The Snowdrops said you was lying naked in the patio of the British Embassy, hollerin' for a dame to massage you. And what you said to the Cultural Attaché wasn't very cultural. Y'told him to . . ." The rest of Hennessey's words were lost in more laughter.

"I tell you I was framed," insisted Morelli. His look of cultivated innocence still didn't fool anyone.

"I won't have any trouble with you this year," said Corrigan. "No liquor."

105

The party lapsed again into silence. They could hear the sound of merry-making from the Soviet sector.

"They've got vodka," said Suki, gnawing a turkey leg. "Pass the Coke."

Rhodes felt guilty. Hidden away under his sleeping bag was the remains of a bottle of gin. He fought a mental battle. His conscience won. He excused himself, went out and returned with an unlabelled bottle. He stood it in front of Corrigan.

"Sorry, that's all there is."

Another wave of laughter reached them from the Russian camp. The Americans were all silent. Their mouths stopped moving. The eyes ranged from the bottle to the Major's face.

"Man, look, hooch," said Hennessey's voice quietly.

"Saki," breathed Suki.

"Grappa," whispered Morelli.

Corrigan stared at the bottle. It'd been a long, dry spell. He uncorked it, and sniffed. "Gin," he said.

He looked at the eyes watching him expectantly.

"Okay, let's kill it." He passed it to Ace. With great ceremony, and with meticulous care, the young Lieutenant measured a tablespoonful of gin into each man's mug.

Albert stared at the thin puddle of liquid at the bottom of his tin cup. This, and the expectancy of the men reminded him of filmed lifeboat scenes when they were doling out the last of the precious water.

Corrigan stood up. "Here's to us."

"In manus tuas commendo spiritum meum," intoned Rhodes. The Marines looked at him, blank-faced. "Into thy hands I commend my spirit," he translated.

The Marines' faces remained expressionless.

"Is that an English joke, sir?" Ace Ellsmore questioned the solicitor.

"Er, yes, I suppose so."

Ace looked round at the still-blank faces of his men. "Okay," he ordered. "Be grateful. Laugh."

They laughed and drank. The American sector of the Island was now truly dry.

The Russians celebrated noisily. It was dark. The fire had been revived and its flames lit the tables and the sitting men.

There were already empty vodka bottles standing like sentinels on the rocks.

The fishermen and scientist chatted, drank and laughed. Vorolokov sat at the apex of the horseshoe of tables. He was as gay as the others. He waved a bottle of vodka and shouted a conversation with Ushakov.

The tables were littered with the remains of the meal. Vorolokov used part of a lobster shell to stub out his cigarette. Glasses clinked. Rasputin lay singeing himself in front of the fire, too fat, too lazy, to move.

There was a rattle of crockery as Igor leapt onto a table, and stood, legs apart, in the firelight, his right arm raised theatrically, holding a glass. It was one of the few occasions when he could legitimately wear his Cossack dress. He loved it. The crew teased him, but secretly understood that these claimed ancestral ties were important to the orphan.

He was a splendid figure in full black trousers and polished boots. An embroidered shirt, with its bloused sleeves, reflected the red firelight. Tucked in the sash was his long silver knife. His wavy black hair was dishevelled. He shook it back out of his eyes.

"To our Captain," he shouted.

He drank, and hurled the empty glass into the fire in the traditional Russian manner.

The others automatically followed suit.

"Igor," bellowed Boris.

"Da?" said Igor.

"They were our only glasses."

Ushakov led the laughter. He reached up and pulled the young Cossack down by his sash. "Then, we will drink out of the bottles, eh, Igor?"

Tanya looked in the direction of the silent American camp.

"They drink quietly, like gentlemen. Not like mad Cossacks," she told Igor.

"They're not drinking at all," he said. "They have no drink."

Vorolokov butted in. "No drink?"

"They told me today they have no liquor."

"Then how do they celebrate their freedom?" asked Sacha.

107

"Coca-Cola," said Igor.

Vorolokov spat into the fire. "Everyone should celebrate with drink. Real drink."

There was a mumur of agreement.

"Everyone should drink on my birthday." Vorolokov thumped himself on the chest and hiccoughed. "We could give them . . ."

"We could ask them . . ." interrupted Tanya.

"Over here . . ." said Ushakov.

"I'll go," shouted Igor in mid-air, as he vaulted the gate. He was already half-way to the American Mess.

His comrades could hear him calling, "Ennessee, Ennessee," as he disappeared behind the American tents.

"Goodbye, beloved Igor," mumbled Boris, crossing himself.

"Ennessee, Ennessee." The Americans looked in surprise towards the Mess door. It exploded open. Morelli, who was balancing on two legs of his chair, fell backwards. Corrigan leaped to his feet as a wild figure of a Cossack appeared, framed in the doorway. It raised its hand. "Peace," said Igor.

Behind him, unnoticed by the Russian, stood the Marine guard, the muzzle of his carbine two inches from Igor's head. The guard looked questioningly at Corrigan. "Peace," said Corrigan, raising his own right hand.

"Three cheers for General Custer," said Clancy Paradise.

"Captain Vorolokov want all come drink his born day," said Igor. Rhodes was already on his feet, but was dragged back into his seat by Victoria, his wig jerked over his forehead.

The eyes, again, all swung towards Corrigan.

"Hummm," he said. "Hummm, why not?"

"Indeed, why not?" asked Rhodes, straightening his hairpiece.

"Thank the Captain. Tell him we will come in five minutes," said Corrigan. There was a cheer. "Have a Coke?" But Igor was gone.

Corrigan put on his stern face. "Now hear this . . . I don't want any trouble. Remember we're their guests. And act like Marines."

"Sure will, sir. We'll drink 'em dry."

Corrigan was alone in the Mess.

By the time he'd passed through the now unguarded gate, the friendly and thirsty Americans were already integrated with their hosts. Hennessey, Igor, Suki and Boris were sitting in a bantering group. Boris's big arm was around Suki's shoulder. The Filipino's head was tilted back. Boris was attempting to pour a half-litre of vodka into the Marine. Suki was doing his best to help him. His eyes popped as he tried to keep up with the flow of spirit. His mouth was overflowing. The vodka ran in dribbles down his neck.

"You haff long way go to catch I," Boris was laughing.

Igor tugged a cork from a bottle with his teeth and handed the vodka to Hennessey.

"Drink and you sing good," he said.

Hennessey's eyes rolled white in the darkness. He kissed the bottle. "There are lots of good songs in a bottle like this." He clamped it to his lips. It gurgled.

Ushakov got to his feet and walked over to the US Major who stood in the shadows, watching the firelit scene. "Please join us."

He led Corrigan over to Vorolokov. "The officer has come," he said.

Vorolokov stood up. He didn't know whether to bow, or offer his hand. He did both.

"Thanks for the invitation," said Corrigan.

Vorolokov put his hand up to silence him. "Please drink with us. My birthday today."

"Happy birthday," said the Major, raising the bottle Ushakov had pressed into his hand. He wondered briefly whether the party was a put up job to lure the Americans over. But the friendliness was obviously genuine. He dismissed the thought.

"How are you together?" Tanya asked Victoria and Albert.

"We've yet to find out," said Albert. He smiled at Victoria.

The three of them sat on a rock by the fire. They shared a bottle.

"You have much men now and many sporting games." Tanya was trying to make small-talk.

109

"Too much of some, not enough of the other." Victoria smiled back at Albert.

Mischa began to play his balalaika. The fisherman sang. The Americans hummed. Zeke went back for his harmonica and the Marines harmonized "Shenandoah".

"Beautiful," sobbed Boris, his eyes streaming.

Victoria slid her hand into the back pocket of Albert's jeans and pushed herself against him. He took a long pull of the vodka.

They sang for an hour, every interval and verse punctuated by the slurping of lips on bottles. The harmony became more venturesome, the tunes more raucous.

"Food," shouted Boris. He appeared with a large steel tray loaded with small roasted birds. He handed them around. There were plenty.

"Geee, midget chickens," said Suki, tearing one apart.

"What d'you call these birds?" Corrigan asked Vorolokov.

"Pigeons," the Russian replied. "I not know Boris had any. Most delicious, aren't they?"

"Hey, mine's got a telephone number on it." Corrigan looked at Morelli who was trying to focus his vodka-blurred eyes.

"What d'you mean?" he asked.

Morelli handed him a small band of metal that he'd pulled off the leg. It read: 4277—US Air Base, Frankfurt.

Corrigan gagged on a half-chewed piece of America's communication system. "We couldn't breed any better ourselves," he said to Vorolokov.

Dishes were cleared away and piled, with empty vodka bottles, on the end table. The men passed around cigarettes, and drank again.

The balalaika came back to life. A slow, sad start, it built pictures of the vast loneliness of the Russian Steppes. Even the Americans found themselves trapped by the haunting notes. It did more than suggest, it told of the plains and the mountains, the winds and the rains. It carried the men with it across great lakes to wild forests and simple villages. It grew. It throbbed as it built towards a crescendo. There was a piercing, ascending whistle from the floodlit bow of the trawler. Startled, they looked up.

Igor's demoniac figure stood, arms akimbo, on the high

bow. His silk sleeves flapped in the warm breeze. With a shrill cry he leapt far out, his feet touching his outstretched hands before he straightened, to land nimbly on the rocks. He whirled, like a Dervish, into the firelight, eyes wide, lips drawn back, teeth reflecting the flames. He translated, into action, the story sung by the balalaika. The music led him faster. He leapt and spun. Cartwheeled and somersaulted. The Russians clapped with the beat of the instrument and drove it even faster. But Igor couldn't be left behind.

The Americans found themselves caught in the fury of the dance. They clapped rhythmically with the Russians and shouted encouragement. Igor, his hair flying, sweat running down his face, kicked his Cossack boots higher.

The music ended abruptly. Igor launched himself high into the air for his finale on the end table. He dropped on one knee, arms wide. The piled crockery, on the other end of the table was catapulted, by his weight, into the darkness. The multiple crash mingled with the ecstatic applause.

"Igor," bawled Boris.

"Da?" panted Igor.

"That was all our crockery!"

The vodka began taking its toll. Boris had succeeded in his self-imposed mission to pour a flask into Suki. He was now working his way through a second bottle. Hennessey was keeping pace.

Ace Ellsmore had already excused himself and was now collapsed in a heap just inside the American sector. Only the promise to his father, never to get drunk on foreign soil, had got him that far. He had crawled the last two yards.

Ushakov and Zeke formed a neat cross where they had fallen together a little way from the fire. Zeke still clutched a near-empty bottle.

Corrigan and Vorolokov, arms around each other's shoulders, were singing two different songs, in two different languages. They thought it sounded harmonious. To Tanya and Victoria, the only two sober ones left, it sounded like two people singing two different songs in two languages.

Rhodes dedicatedly struggled through a fresh bottle. This was where the experienced drinker came out on top. He staggered to his feet, clasped the bottle by its neck and lurched towards the orange tent. He'd finish his vodka in bed.

A lumpy, khaki heap moved slightly in the dull glow of the dying fire on the plateau. It wriggled like a chick trying to escape from its eggshell. It hatched into a swaying, staggering figure, which stumbled towards the American camp. It heaved and crawled its way towards the flagpole and began to pull itself upright against the mast. When finally erect, it fumbled beneath the stained tunic and produced a slightly flattened bugle which it pressed to its lips and blew. Nothing happened. It blew again. The first notes of Taps wavered drunkenly across the Island. They tapered into nothing. The figure made a final effort to remain upright by snatching at the dangling flag halyard. The Stars and Stripes fluttered jerkily down the pole and enveloped him. The bugler collapsed, motionless, formally shrouded by his country's colours.

Albert was swaying on his rock seat. He looked at Victoria and felt an alcoholic wave of desire.

"There's no one else about. Let's get away," he said. "Let's go to the cave."

Victoria pulled him to his feet. He immediately regretted his invitation. The Island spun. He felt he was walking on a gigantic air mattress.

She helped him down across the rocks into the cavern. It was damp and dark, but it was private. It stank.

"Phew," said Albert. His stomach heaved. He felt his way back to the entrance. Victoria pulled him down next to her.

"It always smells here, you'll get used to it. It's probably rotting seaweed."

She kissed him and helped him to undress. Her nervous hands fumbled as she unclipped his belt. He lay on his clothes. She undressed quickly and sat beside him.

Unsteadily Albert reached out and drew her down until he could kiss her breasts.

"Make love to me," she breathed.

She rolled over until he was lying on top of her. He was heavy. Her ribs creaked. This was something the Kama Sutra hadn't warned about. She wriggled to spread his weight, and kissed him hungrily. She could feel his burning body touching along her entire length. She dragged her fingers gently over his back. He seemed to grow heavier.

"Now, darling," she whispered.

Albert fell off.

"Darling?"

Albert's reply was a drunken snore.

If a helicopter of either side had flown over the Island at dawn, a Third World War might have been declared. The two camps looked like a battlefield. Victoria peered out from the orange tent, where she had spent a lonely night. Bodies sprawled everywhere, the still smouldering fire looked like the centre of the holocaust. Men seemed to have staggered away from it in every direction, and then collapsed. They had drunk until daybreak. Empty bottles lay scattered between the bodies.

A few of the Americans had almost made it to their tents. The Russians had met the obstacle of their rope ladder and now made an untidy heap below.

The first sign of life that Victoria saw was the young lieutenant. Ace pushed himself up from the rock and groaned. He looked up and saw Des and Les, the two black cormorants, circling overhead.

"Buzzards," he croaked, and collapsed again.

Albert Ralph Richardson couldn't remember who'd given him back his white feather. He could see it resting on a pebble an inch away from his face. It wavered slightly as he breathed. He could still see; he wasn't blind after all! The sun hadn't yet scorched his optical nerves. There was still a slight chance that he might beat the Fuzzy-Wuzzies and get back to warn the Command. The trouble was that he couldn't remember which Command he was trying to warn, and what it was he should warn about.

Through blurred eyes he saw that he was lying at the entrance to a cave. The sun speared hot darts at his eyes. He reached out for his sun-helmet. He couldn't find it, nor his clothes. He tried to remember the battle where he'd been captured and pegged out in the sun to die. He wouldn't die. Someone must have cut him loose. The white feather ruffled again. Somehow it had got itself stuck on his nose. He blew it off.

Around him lay bodies. He vaguely recognised faces of friends, now dead. He crawled over to one still figure. And painfully rolled it over.

"Massacred," Albert Richardson muttered. "The savages. And all we wanted to do was educate them."

Across the endless miles of tortured rocks, shimmering in the heat, he could see the bright colour of a bedouin tent. "Must get water. Help."

It took him hours to reach the encampment. With a super-human effort, the gallant British officer rose to his feet. A beautiful Arab girl caught him and steered him into the luxurious sleeping quarters. She pushed him, a bit roughly, he thought, onto the silken bed. Everything went black . . .

Victoria had just collected Albert's clothes from the cave, when Tanya shouted from the deck of the trawler.

"Coffee. Come up."

The two girls leaned against the rail of the *Dmitri Kirov* and looked at the devastation below.

"All not living down there," said Tanya.

"Shouldn't we do something?"

"Not do anything. Always like so. Russians drink. Russians fall down. Just leave. Like try on my uniform?"

Victoria realised the reason behind Tanya's invitation. It was a gentle hint she'd like to see Victoria's dresses.

"Come back to my tent," invited Victoria. "You can try some of my clothes, as well."

Tanya liked the short skirts and the feminine colours. When she had put on one of Victoria's bright summer dresses, she pointed questioningly at the make-up case.

The two girls sat together inside the tent while Victoria helped Tanya make up.

"Can I go see in my big mirror?" asked Tanya.

They walked back to the trawler. The dead men were coming slowly back to life. Vorolokov was standing, support-ing himself with the rope ladder. He watched the two girls approach. He shook himself, and rubbed his eyes with the back of his hand. The girls had exchanged heads. "Much too much vodka," he muttered.

Vorolokov looked at Tanya's head on Victoria's body. It was a good combination. He looked for the join at the neck. It had been cleverly done. Unwisely, he let go of the ladder to take her in his arms. He passed out again.

It was evening again before the last of the human debris had made its way back to its quarters. No one spoke. No one ate. The only sounds came from the waves, the occasional calls of the three sea birds and the gentle creaking of the unguarded gate.

It was a familiar sensation that woke Albert, twenty hours later. He rolled over, off his stomach, then quickly rolled back. Gingerly he pushed his hand down until he could feel his behind. "Oh, no," he thought. "Not again!" The tender skin was scorched. He felt sure that it was glowing even in the early dawn light. He couldn't imagine how it had happened. He remembered only one thing since the early stages of the party. He'd had another dream about Victoria. And, as usual, had been interrupted at the crucial moment. This time, instead of there being a cheering audience, a thousand Zulus had thrown him over a cliff.

The camp was already awake. There were cries from the sea where the Marines and fishermen were having an early morning swim. The thought that a dip might cool his burning back drove Albert outside. The camp had already been cleared. With the exception of a blackened piece of rock, there was no indication that the party had ever taken place.

"Oh, so you're alive," said Victoria coolly. "How's lover boy today?"

"Just give me the chance."

"Don't you remember after the party?" she asked. "If you can't, then I won't tell you."

Albert sat in the cooling water and thought. Had he? Did he? Where? When? He vowed never again to get so drunk.

"Ici Paris," said the caller. "What's the latest situation?"

"They're dying," said the Prime Minister.

"Dying?"

"Like flies."

"Like flies?"

"Yes," said the P.M.

"Ze Americans, or ze Russians?" asked the horrified French President.

"Mostly South Americans and one Algerian," replied the P.M.

"Algerian?"

"Yes, it's sagging over the side of the tray. It's the only Aporocactus I've got. Know anything about cactus?"

Bewilderment hushed the line.

"Zey prickle." The Gallic voice was patronising.

"Not mine," said the P.M. smugly, toying with his electric razor.

11

The lethal looking American missile-launcher was a harsh reminder of the former crisis, a possible provocation. To Major Corrigan's aesthetic eye, it was as much out of place against the seascape as a scrap automobile would have been on a Gainsborough. He called the Lieutenant.

"Don't you think the Big Heater is the most beautiful thing that you've ever seen?" he asked him, nodding towards the rocket launcher. "Imagine the thousands of creative hours that were spent on the design."

Ace gave the Major a strange look. "Of course, sir."

"Look at that concerto in alloy," the Major continued. "It takes your breath away. Only a really progressive nation, with its finger on the artistic pulse of civilisation, could produce a masterpiece like that. Don't you agree?"

The Lieutenant gave him an even odder look. "Yes," he said meekly.

"Cover it up," ordered Corrigan. "It spoils the view."

Ten minutes later, the missile launcher was hidden under its olive green cover.

A surprising thing then happened. The Russian scientist appeared on the bow of the trawler. Ushakov looked at the covered missile launcher, and waved a greeting at the Major. Even as Corrigan watched, the phallic Russian rocket, with its scarlet nose-cone, swung down behind the bridge and disappeared. There was a clang as the metal doors of its housing dropped shut. Corrigan smiled thoughtfully.

That evening, he and his Lieutenant shared the same Mess table as Vorolokov and the Russian scientist.

"Today is an historic occasion," said Vorolokov.

"Yes," replied the Major, thinking of the missile incident. "Today we haff done something unique in our memory."

Corrigan began to feel that Vorolokov was becoming over-dramatic.

"We haff drinked our whole year's supply of vodka in our party night. This all we haff left." He waved his hand at the dying bottle, whose level was already below the label. "From tonight, we haff no more drink."

The next morning found the Americans and the Russians sitting on the rocks near the *Dmitri Kirov,* fishing. For most of the Marines, it was their initiation to the sport. They were willing pupils. The Russians taught them how to bait the crab pots, how to lace fish strips onto hooks so that they wouldn't come off. And where to lay the nets and traps. All the Island's boats were commandeered. No sooner was a boat beached, and its crew and catch unloaded, than it was filled again with a fresh batch of enthusiastic tyros itching to get to the virgin fishing ground. The catches were phenomenal. The lobster keep-tank built by the Russians now needed to be enlarged.

Suki and Hennessey scoured the sea bottom with their diving gear and added crawfish to the future menu. The crab pots proved to be irresistible, and the Russians swore that the shellfish were queueing to fill them. Sacha's long gill-net was an embarrassment. When it was strung out for only a few minutes, it trapped a complete shoal of mackerel. The doors of Boris's ice boxes couldn't be closed on the haul.

It seemed logical that the cooks should share the catches, the same cookhouse, and the work. After all, it was only a little more difficult to cater for everyone on the Island in one batch, than it was to cook for the two sectors separately. With a little planning, said Zeke, it would be possible for Boris and he to act as duty cook on alternate days. Boris agreed. It meant that he would be able to get away from the Island with the other fishermen. Anyway, his main concern, at the moment, was his crockery, or more accurately, his lack of it.

They decided that on Mondays, Wednesdays and Fridays, Zeke would feed the Islanders in two sittings. Tuesdays, Thursdays and Saturdays, it would be Boris's turn. Sundays, they would share the work. They put their suggestion to their officers.

"Okay by me," said Corrigan. "Check with the men."

Zeke didn't like the exaggerated enthusiasm with which the Marines greeted the idea.

"Sure suits me," said Suki. "By the way, what d'you call them Russian fish eggs?"

"Caviar," said Zeke.

"D'you boil 'em for two or four minutes?" asked the Filipino.

"Do they put ketchup on shashlik?" queried Morelli, the only uncertain Grunt.

But the idea worked.

The two cooks' ingenuity seemed as unlimited as the fish supply. They competed to prepare the most exotic meals. The islanders became sun-bronzed, well-fed and fitter than they had been in their lives. There was only one thing missing to complete their regal banquets—drink. Even the Coca-Cola supply was getting low.

Rhodes didn't have a hangover. He missed it. The lack of it made him feel ill.

"Daddy, what's the matter?" asked Victoria.

"Post-natal depression," he replied. "I'm sorry I was born."

Like Top Sergeant Hennessey, Rhodes had been a man of habits—but bad ones. He was accustomed to his breakfast gin, his spiritual elevenses, his poured lunch, his toasts at tea-time, sundowners at six, and his bottled dinner that flowed into supper and overflowed into nightcaps. Now he was constrained to food, an unfamiliar experience—trying to his temper and his system. And it wore out his feet. For bad tempered and grumpy he stomped around the Island.

"Zeke," he complained. "I don't know what's wrong with your food, but it's given me blisters. On my feet."

Zeke, who doubled as Medical Corpsman, examined them.

"That sure ain't mah food, Mister. Them blisters is with wearin' tight shoes." Zeke sorted through the medical store and found a bottle of surgical spirit. "Here, rub them feet with this three times a day an' it'll harden 'em up."

Just how or when Rhodes decided to try drinking the surgical spirit, no one on the Island discovered. They found him, after a prolonged search, under the tarpaulin cover of

119

the missile launcher. His face was purple. He was very ill. The surgical spirit bottle was empty. It took Zeke and Ushakov two hours' hard work, first with a stomach pump, and then with quarts of black coffee, to get him on his feet.

A worried group of Rhodes's friends met that evening behind the cookhouse tent.

"This man must haff speerits," said Boris. "When he has speerits he iss sober. When he has no speerits, he iss drunken."

"This mens is inside out to normals peoples," Igor volunteered.

They all nodded in agreement, but nobody, not even Boris really understood what the Cossack meant.

Igor expanded his psycho-analytical prognosis. "Speerit iss to his body like greez to ze engine. Wissout greeze ze engine halt. Wis greez ze engine work good. But it won't alone on ze greez run. Must also haff gasoline food. Meester Rhodes hass gasoline food. But also needs speerits to greez his body engine."

Igor looked triumphantly at the faces around him.

"Sure Igor," said the Lieutenant. The others looked at them blankly. Ace Ellsmore interpreted. "He means that Gin Jim's system is geared to run on hooch."

Igor smiled.

"Gee, Ace, your Russian is sure good," said Morelli.

"So what do we do?" asked Ellsmore.

"I could go to England to get something," offered Albert.

"No good," said Ace. "We've specific orders not to go to the other islands, or to Britain. You can bet by now the coast is crawling with Limey troops."

"What about France?" asked Victoria.

"Yeah." The Lieutenant was silent for a moment. "Yeah," he said again. "No one's actually said we can't to there. Maybe we could bend the rules a little. What about money?"

"The Frenchee must eat feesh," said Boris. "We haff very much feesh. We maybe make exchange feesh wis dreenk."

"Yeah," Ace said a third time.

"We could use your dad's power-boat," said Albert. "It's a fair distance. But we could tow one of the cutters at about twenty knots. I reckon it would take us about five hours."

"I know ze speerits and dreenks good," said Boris.

120

"I keel ze Frenchee an zee greez we stolen after," said Igor.

Albert looked at the Lieutenant. "Do you speak French?" he asked.

"Just a little," replied Ace. "But I don't think I should go."

"Well, I don't speak any French," said Albert. "We could pretend we're just going off fishing. No one'll miss us. We could be back before dark."

"Okay, but if the Major ever found out, he'd break us. If anyone's going to take any risk, it's going to be me. Don't say anything to the others. Don't ask anybody for dollars, or they'll get suspicious."

"Count me in. No one can break me," said Albert.

"We haff plenty feesh now," said Boris. "We put plenty feesh and plenty lobster in box and put in cutter. Tomorrow dawn, you breeng power-boat behind trawler. I put plenty gasoline in cutter for power-boat engine."

It was still dark when Ace Ellsmore, Albert and Victoria crept down the rocks to the power-boat. The Island was silent. They huddled together by the side of the boat. The Lieutenant shone a torch carefully into a valise.

"Think I've got everything I need," he said. "Chart, compass and a bit of money. Did you bring any food?"

"I just raided the cookhouse," said Victoria. "Albert's got some in a plastic bag. Take care. I'll see you tonight. Good luck." She kissed Albert.

"Gee, ma'am," said Ace.

"All right, you as well."

"Just a minute," said a tall voice. Major Corrigan stood close behind them. "Running out on us, uh?"

"N-n-no. No, SIR," said the Lieutenant. "Just going fishing, sir. Er . . . Fishing with Albert."

"What are you hoping to catch this early, Lieutenant?"

"Er, fish, sir . . . dawn fish."

"Dawn fish?"

"The Russians said they're fresher in the morning, sir," stammered Ace.

"And I suppose they'll be smaller, too?"

"Yes, sir. That was what they said, sir. They'd be smaller and fresher . . . er . . . 'cos they're younger." Ace was losing.

121

"They'd have been fresher still yesterday, wouldn't they, Lieutenant? Why didn't you go yesterday?"

"Yesterday I was crab fishing, sir."

"But the crabs would have been bigger if you'd left them until today, wouldn't they, Lieutenant?" Major Corrigan was making snuffing noises in the darkness. Ace hoped he was catching pneumonia.

Victoria interrupted. "You two had better make a move or we won't be getting any dawn fish."

"Yes, you'd better get along," said the Major. "Here, read this when it gets light." He handed Ace a small envelope. "Can't wait to see these dawn fish."

"Yessirrr," Ace thankfully snapped him a salute.

They slid the power-boat stern first into the water. Albert climbed aboard. Victoria threw them the painter and Albert leant his weight against the hull until the bow swung round and pointed out to sea.

"Start up," he called softly.

Ace turned the ignition key. The engine stuttered and fired. Albert climbed into the boat as the Lieutenant put the motor into gear and eased open the throttle. They moved away from the Island. Ace steered the boat round until they were heading towards the trawler. He hoped the Major wouldn't notice. A torch flashed. Ace cut the engine and they coasted onto the beach below the Russian ship. Igor stood in the water next to the cutter. It was heavily loaded. Even in the half light, Albert could see the boxes neatly piled inside.

"Tie it on," said Albert.

Igor and Boris made the cutter fast to the stern of the power-boat.

"Be goink," said Boris. "We come, too. Want help."

Albert watched as the dark bulk of the Island gradually diminished. Within twenty minutes it had disappeared and the rim of the sun fired the horizon ahead of them.

"Take the wheel," said Ace. "I'll check the course."

He pulled out his compass and compared the reading with the small instrument mounted on the power-boat's dashboard. Then he nudged Albert.

"What the hell's going on?" The stern of the power-boat was swinging.

"I'm holding her as steady as I can," Albert shouted back.

Ace looked behind him. Igor was apparently singing to himself. The Lieutenant couldn't hear him, but he could see his mouth opening and closing. The Cossack was lying back against the gunwale of the cutter with his eyes shut. He was operating the tiller with his foot. Swinging it in time to his unheard song.

"Boris, for Christ's sake throw something at Igor," bellowed Ace over his shoulder. There was a thud as Boris heaved a scrubbing brush at the young Russian. The swinging stopped. Boris waved his fist at the stern.

"Thought you might be in trouble with the Major," said Albert. He'd just enjoyed a couple of minutes imagining himself as Captain Albert Bligh and flogging Igor all round the fleet.

"I *was* in trouble with the Major. Thank heaven he believed me."

"What was the envelope?"

Ace felt in his pocket and pulled out the crumpled letter. He opened it.

"What is it?"

"A ten dollar bill and a message."

"What's it say?"

"It says . . ." Ace gulped. "And get me a bottle of brandy at the same time!"

The sun rose, a dull red tomato on the horizon away to their left. The sea was almost smooth. The two boats made good time towards their destination. There was no land in sight, in any direction.

The motor ran smoothly. But it was noisy, and conversation was difficult. Albert detected an apparent slight change in the engine note. He looked round. It was Boris. Asleep and snoring. Igor was now sitting astride the tiller bar of the cutter, steering by leaning one side or the other. He was peering ahead looking for the first sight of France.

"Food," shouted Ace. "Change places."

Albert half stood, while Ace wriggled into the driving seat and took the controls. Albert untied the plastic bag given to him by Victoria. He pulled out a handful of thick sandwiches. The rocking of the boat as Ace and Albert changed places had disturbed Boris. He was now awake. Albert passed him some food.

"What about Igor?" Albert asked Boris.

"Give me his feed," said the Russian cook.

Albert passed him Igor's sandwich. Boris put it on top of his own and ate the two together.

"Him too fat," he said. "Anyway, him fish."

Albert looked round at Igor again. The Cossack was fishing. As Albert watched, he began pulling in a long line he was trailing behind the cutter. As it drew nearer the boat, Albert could see the flash of a mackerel that had taken the young Russian's metal spinner.

"He catch more grease," said Boris with a wink.

Igor unhooked the fish and dropped it into the top of the nearest box. Then he threw the line back into the sea. His enthusiasm for fishing was endless. It took him three hours to top up all the boxes. There were even a few fish sliding around by his feet.

"Franchee!" shouted Boris. He was standing up behind Albert, supporting himself by holding Albert's shoulders. "Franchee! Look."

Ahead showed a low dark streak misting above the water. Albert could just make out the low coastline.

"We're almost there."

Ace smiled. "Trust the Marines."

"With everything except women," replied Albert.

The land mass grew until they could distinguish sand dunes and wooden breakwaters. There were clusters of coloured tents among the sand hills. Small black dots that sprinkled the beaches became sunbathers as the boat drew nearer. Away to the right were the terra-cotta roofs of a small fishing town.

Ace consulted his chart. "That's the Ville de Roche, near Argenton. How's that for navigation?"

"I thought you were aiming for Brest," said Albert.

Ace flushed. "This is nearer," he said. "Head for the beach. We don't want to go through the port, or we'll be caught by customs."

"It looks like a campsite."

"All the better," said Ace. "They'll just think we're fishermen."

The water was shallowing. There were swimmers. Ace slowed the engine and trickled the boat towards the beach. They nosed it in gently. The cutter caught up with them and rammed the power-boat firmly into the sand.

There seemed to be suntanned girls in assorted stages of undress lying in untidy rows on every sand dune as far as they could see.

Igor whistled and called something to Boris in Russian. Boris tut-tutted.

"My navigation must be better than I thought," said Ace. "This must be heaven." Albert was too interested to say anyting. He hadn't seen as many girls as this since Eddie Cantor's Roman Scandals was shown at Manny's Biograph three months ago.

"I'll go over and try my French," said Ace. He stepped out of the boat.

By the time he got to the most attractive group, all the girls on the beach were sitting up, watching. The more undressed ones were hastily tying on bikini tops.

"Bonjour, Madamoiselle, comment ça va?" he began. The pretty, dark-eyed brunette looked up at him, then turned to her friend.

"Ain't he the cutest, Thelma?" she said. She swivelled back to him: "We not speak French," she said loudly, and slowly.

"Oooph," said Ace. He walked back to Albert.

"My navigation couldn't be this bad," he said. "She's a Texan, probably from Dallas. And she thinks I'm a Frenchie. Now what do we do?"

"Try that group over there," said Albert.

A hundred and sixty soft eyes watched the embarrassed Lieutenant as he made his way over to the group Albert had pointed out.

He began his speech again.

"Sorry, fella, I don't speak your lingo . . ."

Ace, even more red-faced and embarrassed, returned to the boat again. "A New Englander this time. What we going to do? We daren't let them know we're not French, otherwise they may give the game away. And we haven't got a passport between us."

Boris and Igor came over. The four of them mapped out a plan of campaign as they sat in the power-boat.

"The only thing to do," Ace said to Boris, "Is for you and Igor to speak to the girls in English. They'll think your accent's some kinda French. Al and I will pretend we don't understand English. We've got to find out where the fish market is."

The four of them strolled over to the Dallas group, and squatted in front of them.

"Why you not much meat?" Igor asked the slim brunette.

"Charming," she drawled. "The subtle Continental approach slays me."

Boris sank his elbow deep into Igor's diaphragm and effectively silenced him. "We wish sell feesh in market," he began. "You tell where is market, pliss?"

"Sorry. Didn't know there was one here. We're just camping."

Ace leaned over and whispered in Boris's ear.

"Is all peoples here American?" the cook asked.

"Sure, we're all together. We're on a students' vacation."

The girls had now been joined by two dozen of their companions. They stood or sat around in a close circle, watching the visitors. Ace became increasingly conscious of the perfume and the smell of the sun oil.

"Isn't the slim one dishy?" said a young redhead.

"Lay off — I saw him first," snapped Dallas.

"The Slavic-looking one's more handsome. He's sexy," said another. "And anyway the thin one needs fattening."

"I wouldn't mind looking after him," said a blonde.

"I wonder if they've got tattoos," giggled the plumpest of the girls.

"Not above the waist, as far as I can see," said another.

Ace was apprehensive about the direction the conversation was taking. The remarks were becoming more and more personal.

"Girls, girls. What are you doing?" A matronly voice came to the men's rescue.

"We think they're trying to sell fish, Miss Baedecker. But we can't understand what they're saying," said Dallas.

Miss Baedecker turned to Boris: "Qu'est-ce que vous faites?" she asked in perfect French. Ace was impressed by

Boris's reaction. The big cook kept his bent face completely expressionless, and answered the woman with a long sentence in Russian.

"Oh, dear." Miss Baedecker looked at the girls with distress. "They seem to speak some local dialect. Maybe it's Basque. I can't understand a word."

Boris pressed his advantage and, taking the woman's arm, he spoke more slowly and even louder—in Russian.

Miss Baedecker was flustered.

"Try English," said Dallas. "I think fatty was trying to speak it before."

Miss Baedecker looked relieved. She hitched up her floppy grey slacks that reminded Albert of the rear end of a stage elephant. "What can I do for you?" she asked.

Boris explained again, in laborious English, that they wanted to find the fish market to sell their cargo.

Miss Baedecker translated each of Boris's words, into American, as he spoke.

"We wanting," said Boris.

"They want," said Miss Baedecker.

"Finding," said Boris.

"They want to find."

"Feeshing selling place." Boris took a deep breath.

"They want to find a fish market."

"Marvellous," said Dallas. "We knew that ten minutes ago."

"For to selling feesh."

"To sell their fish," said Miss Baedecker, triumphantly.

"What did you think they were, white-slavers?" asked Dallas.

"Hush, girls."

"Say, Miss Baedecker, couldn't we buy their fish off them. I'm getting awful sick of pork, beans and ice-cream," said the plump girl.

"It might be cheaper than buying from the town, at that," said the broad-hipped matron. She turned to Boris. "How many dollars for your fish?" she asked.

"Dollars?"

Ace pulled him aside. "A dollar's just about the same as a rouble."

"Ah," said Boris. He stood up and walked down to the

boat, making a careful estimate of the amount of fish and their approximate value in the Russian markets. At last he returned.

"Sixty dollars," he beamed.

Miss Baedecker assumed her bargaining expression. "That's far too much."

Boris now looked horrified. He threw his arms up into the air and hit himself on the head with the palms of his hands.

"Sixty dollar, much feesh."

"Forty dollars," said Miss Baedecker firmly.

Boris turned to Igor and spoke in Russian. Igor uttered a heart-rending cry and hid his face in the crook of his elbow. Boris turned back to Miss Baedecker.

"I tell him you rob his children," he said. The big cook turned to Albert and again spoke in Russian. Albert followed Igor's lead and beat himself on the chest, at the same time trying to look as anguished as possible. It was difficult.

"What on earth . . . ?" began Miss Baedecker.

"Man is sad. He know old mother soon go heaven. No food," said Boris. "Sixty dollars?"

"Forty-five dollars," said Miss Baedecker.

Boris turned to Ace. He patted him kindly on the shoulder, looked hard into his eyes, and spoke softly in Russian. Ace almost exploded trying to conceal his laughter. He, too, covered his face and made loud sobbing noises.

"This one sick wife. No money, no doctor. Wife perhaps die yesterday." Boris had great tears running down his cheeks. He was so emotionally involved in his bargaining that he nearly believed his own sad stories. He slumped down on the sand, pulled up the hem of his thick sweater and dabbed at his eyes. "Sixty dollar?"

Miss Baedecker was visibly shaken. Through his parted fingers, Albert could see tears forming in her eyes. She sniffed.

Boris continued, unrelenting. He spoke again to Igor. The young Cossack limped clumsily towards the boat, returning a moment later with a crate of lobsters. As he approached, Boris nodded his head towards him.

"Very bad accident. Was ballet dancer. Now poor lame

feeshman. Broke leg falling over bouquet. No pension. Sixty dollar?"

"Fifty dollars," conceded Miss Baedecker. Her lip trembled.

"Now maybe we start bargain," said Boris. "I make price come down. You make price come up. Fifty-nine and half dollar?"

They settled at fifty-eight dollars. The American chaperone unbuttoned a money belt and counted the clean bills into Boris's oily hand. "Please carry the fish up to our cooking tent," she told him.

Igor forgot his limp as he hurried to unload the crates. Albert and Ace helped him, and together they carried the boxes up into the sand dune camp.

"Which way town?" Boris asked Dallas.

The girl pointed.

"You stay here tonight?" she asked Ace.

He pretended not to understand. Dallas turned to Boris. "Are you all staying here tonight?"

"No, we go. Must go back to feesh fleet. Not stop."

Dallas sighed.

The four men walked along the sand track towards the town. The sun was overhead. The hot sand filled their sneakers. Half a mile on, the track reached a narrow tarmac road.

The town was bigger than it had appeared from the sea. The tall, shuttered houses stretched back inland, on either side of a steep walled harbour. Boris and Igor looked down on the moored fishing boats with professional eyes. Ace pulled them away.

"Don't do anything that will attract attention," he warned. "Let's find somewhere to buy the wine."

The main street was filled with people. They seemed to be a mixture of holidaymakers and local inhabitants. Below the bunting and flags, they stood around expectantly, as though they were waiting for a carnival to begin.

"Wonder what's going on?" asked Albert.

"Probably a religious festival," replied Ace.

Buying the wine wasn't quite as easy as they had previously imagined. The small general stores didn't seem to carry large stocks.

129

"A hundred bottles? Sorry, we are almost sold out. We have only twenty, but plenty of draught wine if you have your own bottles."

"We've got to have a collecting point," said Ace. "If we keep together it's going to take us a day to get all we want. Boris, tell Igor to wait on the crossroad near the entrance of the town and to guard the wine we bring him."

They divided the money, and then headed in different directions into the narrow streets.

The pile of crates and miscellaneous bottles grew around Igor. It was thirsty work. He levered the cork out of a bottle with his fishing knife and sat on the top of the crates. He was about to lift the wine to his mouth, when a cyclist appeared round the corner of the road behind him. The man was working hard, standing on the pedals to get maximum speed from his machine. His canary yellow sweater glowed in the sun.

He lifted his head momentarily as he approached Igor.

Igor was swigging at the wine when the cyclist reached him. The bottle was snatched from Igor's hand. With an angry yell he looked up. The thief was speeding away, the bottle held high to his lips as he drained it. Then it was thrown empty over a hedge.

Igor worked the cork out of another bottle. He had just started drinking, when a second cyclist, this time in a red sweater, with matching cap, reached him. This flagon was also snatched, drained and discarded.

A third litre was similarly stolen before Igor hustled the crates to the side of the road and covered them with long grass. He had only just hidden them, when dozens of riders appeared, accompanied by a honking, hooting crocodile of television vans, cars and motorcycles. They swept past the Russian, leaving him astonished and dust-covered.

"Fantastic," Boris chuckled to Igor, while the four men sat counting the bottles an hour later. "We were standing down by the harbour, when Albert heard that this Tour de France cycle race was due to pass us. Then, the first of the riders came down the hill—drunk. He circled the pisshouse

130

twice and then rode straight into the harbour. We nearly died laughing.

"The man next to me thought the rider had got sunstroke. Then the second cyclist came along. He was drunk, too. He was singing. He took the wrong turning in the town and disappeared down a road that leads only to the sea.

"But the third rider ... he stopped in the middle of the town and relieved himself against the stage where the Mayor and his wife were standing. Then he was sick. He started to get back on his cycle, but collapsed. The gendarmes took him away. We had to wait until the other riders came through before we could get past the crowds and back here."

Igor decided to keep quiet about the wine bottles.

"Did you get the brandy?" Albert asked Ace.

"Could I ever forget that? Got a bottle in my pocket."

Between them, they carried the crates, in stages, back down the sandy road to the beach. It seemed twice as far as they remembered.

The last two hundred yards were easy, the girls were still sunbathing and seemed pleased to be able to help them.

"Going to have a party?" Dallas asked Boris.

"No, just wine for feesh fleet." Boris hoped she wasn't going to ask about the money they'd got on behalf of their sick dependants.

"Can't you go back tomorrow? Tell them you had bad weather or something." She talked to Boris, but looked at Ace.

"Sorry, must go feesh fleet now." Boris was adamant. Ace was beginning to wonder if, perhaps, they would be missed for another evening. But he realised that if they didn't get back, Corrigan would certainly start a search for them. If he got really worried he might even alert the Sixth Fleet — then there'd be trouble.

They loaded the cutter in silence.

"Come back sometime and stay longer," shouted Dallas as they pulled away from the beach. Soon, the shore merged into the land mass and France was well behind them. Ahead, the boats of the French fishing fleet were scattered. Ace chose a course to take them clear of the long nets that trailed behind the drifters.

131

The hardest part of the expedition was over. The men were jubilant as they discussed the day's masquerade.

Albert laughed. "Your parents must have been Arabs, your bargaining was perfect, Boris. I don't think I'll ever believe you again."

Boris laughed with him. "I sorry making all peoples families sick. But best humour was bicycle race. In France it is most funny sport. In Russia, most serious."

It was three o'clock. The sea was still calm, the weather hot. Ace checked his tides again and altered course so that when the direction of the current changed later, it would help in the final run towards Foul Rock.

Everyone was happy. There was a shout from Igor in the rear boat. He waved a wine bottle at them and then tossed it forward to Boris. The cook drove the cork in with the blade of a screwdriver and took a long pull before passing it on to Ace and Albert. They emptied the bottle and then opened another. Albert threw Igor the remainder of the sandwiches.

They were now level with the French fishing boats. Boris waved to the men working on a drifter. They waved back. The outboard engine coughed, spluttered and died.

"Gasoline," said Ace. "Igor, pass the spare cans."

"Spare cans?" repeated Igor. He looked embarrassed.

"Igor," said Boris threateningly. He said something in Russian.

The Cossack stammered and blushed. "Gasoline, I, er. I take out cans to put in more feesh. I sorry."

"You what?" bawled Ace.

"I forgot put back," said Igor.

Boris lumbered to his feet, almost upsetting the boat. He dragged the cutter towards him by the painter, then jumped across the narrowing gap. He roared. He went berserk. He grabbed the unfortunate Cossack with both hands, lifted him off his feet and threw him backwards into the sea. He seized an oar ready to smash down on Igor's head as he surfaced.

"Boris," shouted Albert. "Don't."

Boris looked round at Albert and let the oar drop back into the bottom of the boat. "Yes, okay," he growled. "Far better not to beat over head. Best let him drown slow like you say."

Igor rose, gasping, to the surface.

"Get him back in," said Ace.

"If he come back, he row us all way to Island," said Boris.

"I row, I row," spluttered Igor.

Albert reached out and caught him by the shoulders of his sweater, and pulled him up onto the gunwale. Igor rolled over into the boat.

"I row good," he promised.

"No use," said Ace. "We don't stand an earthly chance of getting back by rowing. We've got to get gasoline. Maybe we can get some off the fishing boats."

"I go," said Igor.

"No!" said three voices simultaneously.

"This time I'm doing it myself," said Ace. He climbed over into the cutter and untied the painter.

Boris shuffled himself a seat on the boxes in front of Ace and dropped the oars into their rowlocks. His broad back strained. They headed for the nearest fishing boat.

The French fishermen had seemed friendly when they had waved to them from the power-boat. They weren't so friendly when it came to giving twenty gallons of fuel away.

Albert could hear the voices from 100 yards away. He couldn't see the cutter, it was hidden behind the fishing boat. Half an hour later, it reappeared.

"How did you get on?" he shouted to Ace.

"We got the bloody gas. But we had to trade the wine."

"All of it?"

"Damned near."

"Oh, Christ."

They refilled the fuel tank and pumped the first of the gasoline through to the carburrettor. The engine started easily.

No one spoke. Igor sat slumped in the back of the power-boat. Now, he wasn't even allowed to steer the cutter. Boris decided that he would do it himself. Ace rechecked his course.

The sun was just setting when they reached the Island. Victoria, Corrigan, Morelli, Rhodes and Collins were standing on the rocks.

"Good trip? Get any dawn fish?" shouted Morelli as the boat headed towards the mooring.

For the first time in his life, Ace swore in front of a lady, and his Commanding Officer. "Balls," he said.

Meanwhile, in Downing Street, the red telephone hummed attention. The P.M.'s secretary picked it up.

"The Vatican?"

"Then it must be a crossed line," the P.M. called over.

The secretary listened to the sepulchral Italian voice, and replaced the receiver.

"No, it's about your cactus. They heard from Paris. They said bury it for three days, then sprinkle it with holy water, how's your wife, and hung up."

The P.M. carefully wrote his name on a dead cactus with his ball-point and buried it with his plastic tea-spoon.

"I'll soon show 'em," he muttered.

12

Eight bottles of wine, and Corrigan's bottle of brandy, was all that was brought back by the Igor-fated expeditionary force. It lasted the Islanders exactly twenty-seven minutes. A glass a man before their evening meal, a large brandy apiece for the officers, a coke for Igor. And the Island was dry again.

"Say, Kentucky," shouted Morelli across the table to Zeke. "Bet your ol' pappy wouldn't stay short of liquor. We'd be bathin' in moonshine if you was a real hillbilly."

There was a sudden silence around the long table.

"What'd I say?" asked Morelli.

"Say it again," said Suki.

"What'd I say?" repeated Morelli.

"No, you spaghetti-haired wop, the first part."

"About the moonshine?"

"Yeah. A still," said Suki. "Could you do it, Zeke?"

"Guess so," said Zeke. He suddenly looked more interested. "Sure Ah could. Boy, could Ah! A still. Git me a piece of paper. Ah'll draw one. Ah'll show you what Ah need. We could build us a beaut. And not an excise man in sight."

Zeke's drawing was complicated. His list of requirements was long, but his helpers were enthusiastic.

"I've seen a piece like that on the jeep," said Clancy.

"I can make one of them easy," said Morelli.

"All we need is junk," said Suki.

"I'll sit and watch it all day long," promised Gin Jim Rhodes hopefully. "I'm sure I'm cut out to be a distiller." He twitched his wig back into place.

"Okay," said Corrigan. "You make a still. Keep it hidden and out of the way. But I'll ration the drink—all of it. Understand? No blackmarket and no secret drinking. Every-

135

body helps. Everybody gets the same amount a day. And each man's ration gets drunk at the time of issue. No storing."

"What'll you use for the mash?" asked Rhodes.

"Easy," replied Zeke. "Ah can use any vegetables. Potatoes, potato peelings, cabbage stalks, cans of fruit, anything. It'll all go in together. An' ah bet Boris has got plenty of scraps, too. An' if we need extra vegetables, well, we get the fly boys to drop us more. Ah'll tell 'em we suddenly got a lot of vegetarian Grunts."

Reveille on the Island was now 11 a.m.—if the bugler was awake in time, or not out fishing. But the following morning it was early, 9.30 a.m. Rhodes, with wild enthusiasm, went round the tents, and rousted the Marines. He was in high spirits.

"Major's parade in ten minutes," he said.

It was probably the strangest assembly in American Marine history. There wasn't a carbine in sight. Not a single pair of polished boots. In fact, only the Lieutenant was wearing boots. And they looked incongruous with his Bermuda shorts and pyjama jacket. He decided that, as this was the first parade for more than two weeks, he should also wear his field service cap with its rank bar. Nobody else wore anything resembling Government Issue. None of the Marines had gone as far as growing beards. Most wore swimming briefs and sneakers.

Hennessey had adopted Igor's black astrakhan hat. It matched his crinkly black hair perfectly. His head looked flat-topped and a foot taller. Morelli wore Rhodes's cycling cap, back to front. It was the nearest thing he could find to a baseball cap.

" 'Shun," shouted Ace, as the Major stepped out of his tent.

Corrigan wrapped his red silk dressing gown tighter around him, and paced, his hands behind his back, up and down the ranks of Marines. He stopped in front of Suki.

"What are you supposed to be," he asked.

Suki puffed out his bare chest, pulled in his chin, and stared straight ahead.

"You're a Marine," Corrigan went on. "Don't forget that. If you're going to wear a Marine Corps badge, make sure it's clean."

"Badge, sir?" queried Suki, glancing down at his only item of clothing, his swimming shorts.

"What's that on your chest?" Corrigan prodded the Filipino's tattoo.

"Oh, that badge, sir?"

"Yes," said the Major. "Get it clean. It's got egg on it."

Corrigan eyed his weirdly-dressed team.

He strode to the flagpole, turned and addressed them.

"The US Marine Corps has a long tradition as one of the most efficient machines in anyone's army. I want that tradition upheld. Recently, there have been a number of independently organised missions which have turned out to be little more than abortive fiascos. This will not happen again. From now on, I am going to organise . . ."

"The abortive fiascos?" asked a voice.

"Thank you, Marine Morelli, for volunteering for latrine duties for the next week," the Major continued.

"As I was saying, from now on I am going to organise everything we do on this island. If we go fishing, it'll be in an organised, efficient manner. If we sunbathe, it'll be in disciplined, tidy lines. If we play baseball, we're going to stick to the rules. And when we build this still, we'll do it in military fashion. Nothing's to be left to chance. Got that?"

"Sir," said the Lieutenant.

"Sergeant Hennessey has orders how I want this camp run. He'll tell you them after parade. Meantime, I want volunteers with a knowledge of engineering and carpentry. Report to me in the Mess.'

Most of the Russian fishermen had wandered over to see what was going on. They stood and lounged around, watching on the edge of the parade ground. When Ace dismissed the men, Boris and Ushakov walked over to him.

"What's a still?" asked Ushakov.

"Equipment for making alcohol."

"Alcohol?"

"Sure, we're going to make our own hooch."

"That's dangerous, unless you really know what you doing," said the Russian scientist. "You have chemist with you?"

"No, but we have Zeke. They make a lot where he comes from."

137

"I think I'd better speak to Major Corrigan," said Ushakov.

He walked to the queue growing outside the Mess. The Major saw him and beckoned him in.

"Hi, Usha. What can I do for you?"

"I wish to help with your alcohol. I have experience of this at university. Much can go wrong if care is not taken. Temperature is most critical. Otherwise you get fusel oil which can kill or blind."

"You're on," said Corrigan. "We'll make you chief distiller. I'm sure Gin Jim will understand."

Ushakov looked thoughtful. "I think," he said slowly, "I know where we should build the still. There is in the cave a small natural gas seepage. This makes the bad smell. We can use the gas to fire the boiler. Also we have much copper pipe aboard the *Kirov*, and welding guns."

"Great," said Corrigan. "We'll build the still. You run it."

He looked at the scientist, smiled and added: "You don't know much about American Marines."

"No," confessed Ushakov.

"They're the horniest, toughest soldiers we've got. They'll only listen to their officers." He looked up and signalled Hennessey. "Sergeant," he said, "I want you to make it clear to all the men that Professor Ushakov is now an honorary captain in the US Marine Corps. He'll see to it that nothing goes wrong with the distilling. He'll be obeyed absolutely as far as this operation is concerned."

Boris took over the cooking for the time it took to build the still. Zeke was fully occupied as technical adviser to the engineers. There was considerable cannibalisation of the *Dmitri Kirov*. Temperature gauges disappeared from the engines. The welding guns were again lowered from the trawler's deck and sparks flew from burning metal.

Zeke was a perfectionist. Every joint was carefully brazed on the large copper boiler. One of his pressure cookers was adapted to make an air-tight lid for the main container. Gleaming copper condensation pipes twisted their way out of the top of the boiler and were fed, in a large coil, through a sea-water cooling tank. From there, they ran down to the alcohol collecting point where the liquid would be caught in bottles.

The huge gleaming apparatus was supported on adjustable

legs over the fissure in the rock from which the gas was leaking. Temperature was to be controlled by the height of the still above the fire. A small hand-pump led fresh sea-water up to the cooling tank. Another rubber hose led the waste water away.

Cables from the trawler carried electricity to light the cave. And an ingenious air conditioning plant, driven by a tyreless wheel of the jacked-up jeep, blew fresh air to the back of the cavern. It was a masterpiece in moonshine engineering. Zeke's family would have been proud to have owned it. And, finally, in true moonshiner manner, the cave was camouflaged with the Marine's netting, rocks, small boulders and seaweed.

While the still was being completed, Boris made the mash to Zeke's instructions. It fermented in sterilised drums on the leeward side of the island. Every scrap of waste vegetable matter went into the cans. After a couple of days, they bubbled away volcanically in the hot sun.

The making of the still was the first big co-operative exercise in the Island's history. Even those not actively involved in its building, or the preparation of the mash, couldn't be kept away. They came, like expectant fathers to witness the birth of their raceless child. There were so many, at times, that Ushakov rationed visiting hours, as the rubber-necking interfered with the work.

Finally, the still was ready. The interior of the cave now looked more like a clinic than a grotto. The white-washed walls reflected the bright light of the fluorescent tubes. The polished copper shone, its surface unmarked by so much as a fingerprint. The floor was levelled and covered with coconut matting. Ushakov stood, his eyes gleaming, beside the still, like some mad scientist with his tame monster.

"Right," he told Zeke. "I think it's ready to work. Get the mash."

The first drum was rolled into the cave and its contents ladled into the boiler. It stank even worse than the gas outlet. Ushakov checked the mash level, and tightened down the lid.

"Get the Major," he said.

Corrigan came excitedly down to the cave.

"Ready to light the gas," said Ushakov. "It is your honour."

The men called to each other and gathered in silence at the entrance to the cave. All the Island's inhabitants were present.

"Speech," said Gin Jim Rhodes.

"You should make it," said Corrigan.

Rhodes cleared his throat and adjusted his wig. He turned to the crowd. "In the history of every country," he began, "there is a moment when true civilisation is realised . . ."

"Light the fire," interrupted a voice from the crowd. Rhodes ignored it.

"This Island should be renamed Elysium. The first country in the world to devote its total manpower, its entire resources and objectives to the production of that balm of the human soul, alcohol."

"Fer Christ's sake light the flame," insisted the voice.

Rhodes reached into his pocket and pulled out his cigarette lighter. He held it at arm's length and flipped the catch. Corrigan rolled a fat spill of paper and held it to the weak flame. The men held their breath.

The Major turned, stooped and tossed the taper beneath the still. There was a whoosh as the gas ignited. A blue flame kissed the sides of the copper boiler. Its burnished walls dulled. The crowd cheered. Ushakov smiled in a professional way.

"Something's missing," said Clancy.

"What?"

"The three wise men."

The crowd were reluctant to leave the cave. They sat in the warm evening air, on the rocks, outside the entrance. They knew it would be hours before the first drop of spirit fell from the end of the copper pipe into the bottle, but they wanted to be there when it happened. They sat and sang softly to Mischa's balalaika. Boris brought over trays of coffee and thick ham sandwiches. The jeep engine chugged on. The warm air that now blew from the cave had lost its objectionable smell. It smelt of boiling cattle food. To Rhodes, it was perfume.

"Watch the temperature most carefully," said Ushakov.

"Too low and we won't get anything. Too high and it will be spoilt."

Zeke sat, his eyes on the temperature gauge. "It's right now," he said.

"Hold it like that," Ushakov told the crew. They jacked up the still legs slightly as the temperature rose a fraction. It dropped back to the red line the scientist had painted on the dial. "Good," he said.

"Look, everybody," shouted Suki. "Look here." He pointed to the end of the copper pipe that ran into the bottle. There was a scuffle outside the entrance to the cave as men tried to push their way in. "Look," said the excited Suki again. They looked. A small drop of clear liquid was beginning to form. It swelled slowly. It grew until it swung gently on the end of the pipe. Finally, it fell noiselessly to the bottom of the bottle A second began to form.

There was a cheer from the men.

"Ah," said Rhodes. "Nectar."

The drip became a dribble. The bottom of the bottle was covered. It began to fill. By morning, they had three bottles.

"Tested it yet?" asked Rhodes, who'd allowed himself two or three hours' sleep. The distilling crew had worked right through the night.

"Not yet," said Ushakov. "Soon I will test."

Corrigan and Rhodes carried the three bottles out into the daylight. It felt cold outside after the clammy hotness of the cavern. They stood the bottles on a flat rock.

"It looks all right," said Corrigan.

"Will be too strong," said Ushakov. "Get me glass please."

He poured a tumbler of the clear liquid and then drew a small hydrometer out of the breast pocket of his white coat. He lowered it into the glass. Like a doctor taking a reading from his thermometer, he studied the instrument.

"Ninety-nine point six degree alcohol," he said. "Very good. Very pure. But much too strong. We must make it weaker by half. Like this it will dehydrate fatty tissue in throat and stomach."

"Ah've got grapefruit juice, an' pineapple juice, an' tomato juice, an' condensed milk, an' Coca-Cola," said Zeke. "We can make it in plenty of flavours."

"We'll settle for the fruit juices," said Corrigan.

They poured the spirit back into its bottle and carried the liquor over to the Mess. Fifteen minutes later, they had six bottles of drink. Two of each of the fruit flavours. The tasting committee consisted of the distilling crew, Ushakov, Corrigan and Rhodes. They poured a small glass for each man.

"I try," said Ushakov. He sipped his glass, then tossed it down in one gulp. "Still strong," he said. "But is good."

The others tried theirs. The liquid had a slightly musty flavour but it was drinkable. And it was strong.

"Must be stronger than gin," said Rhodes, his eyes watering.

"Stronger than bourbon," said Corrigan.

"What about another?" asked Suki.

"How much of this stuff do you reckon you can turn out each day," asked Corrigan.

"Six to eight," said Ushakov.

"Right. Let's ration ourselves to two tots a day until we've stockpiled a few bottles."

Not even Rhodes opposed this idea.

Guards and security checks came back to Foul Rock that night. But it wasn't the frontier they were protecting. It was their Aladdin's Cave. The Russians and the Americans worked it in turn. They took their duties as seriously as they had while guarding the barrier. No one, apart from Ushakov and Corrigan, went into the cave without an official pass. Even the work teams were searched on the way out.

Night guard duties became popular, because the guards earned an extra tot of liquor at midnight. The rest of the Islanders got one tot with their morning coffee, and one as a nightcap. They drank to Corrigan's regulations. There was no hoarding. Gradually the stocks of liquor in the cave grew, and the rations increased. By the end of the first week, there was a cellar of almost sixty bottles of the fruit-juice brandy.

Corrigan's biggest difficulty was in deciding how the liquor should be dispensed. He didn't want the men to have too easy access to it. He couldn't sell it for cash. Many of the men had no money. He discussed the problem with

Vorolokov. The Russian solved the problem. He suggested that every job and chore on the Island should be allocated points, and that, in turn, the points would buy a glass, a half-bottle or a bottle of liquor. Catching a lobster earned five points, and five points was worth a glass. Half a stone of mackerel equalled one lobster. Emptying the latrines was equal to catching two lobsters. Two nights' work on the still was enough for a half-bottle of liquor. All the normal duties and jobs around the camp had their reward in points.

It was the still that caused the Island to become a truly democratic state. The officers felt that they, too, should earn their points, but they weren't sure how they should go about it. Collins made a suggestion.

"It's been obvious for a long time that we need a council to run things. There's too much duplication of work."

Vorolokov and Corrigan looked at him. They had just finished dinner, and were having a nightcap.

"As far as the ship and this military camp are concerned, the officers carry on as usual. But the well-being of the community as a whole is really the job for a committee. Why don't we appoint one?"

No one could think of a reason. They agreed to an election. Collins passed around blank pieces of paper and everybody was asked to nominate two candidates.

It was something of a relief to both Corrigan and Vorolokov that they were elected, as were Hennessey and Ushakov. The council of four held their first meeting—in public. They sat at a long table on the plateau, the Islanders on the rocks around them. It was a formal gathering. at which they decided to elect a chairman, with a casting vote. They chose Albert. Collins became a co-opted member as Clerk of the Council.

They explained to the Islanders the full purpose of the committee. Military duties apart, they would rule everything, and this particularly included the still. Misdemeanours, complaints, and suggestions would all be dealt with by the Council. They would draw up a rota of point-earning duties to be done, to avoid the possibility of anyone monopolising the chores earning most marks. At the suggestion of Sacha, the Council agreed to the award of initiative points. These would go to men or women who originated ideas to improve the living conditions.

Vorolokov made the first gesture, by offering the use of his trawler's hot showers to the Westerners.

"We also extend to you our Mess and permit free run of our ship. However, there certain private sections which I ask you not visit. These I will mark."

Corrigan thanked the Russian skipper. "I guarantee your wishes will be respected. In return, we offer to you the hospitality of this end of the Island."

To Rhodes, this was clearly only a formality. For the past couple of weeks, the men had come and gone as they'd pleased.

The system worked well. There was plenty of time for leisure in the late July sun. There was always a surplus of cookhouse orderlies to help Zeke and Boris. The Island became tidy. Working parties hauled the loose boulders off the plateau, dragged rocks out of a swimming area, and cleared the coastline of unsightly seaweed. Disciplined fishing parties kept the trawler's refrigerators crammed. A mooring jetty was built. Sports were organised. Lev, who was the trawler's carpenter, laminated water skis for Ace, who started a daily skiing class.

The humorous highlight of every day was the after-lunch judo lessons Suki gave to Igor. The young Cossack was an apt pupil, but nobody was sure whether the lessons were intended to teach Igor, or merely to keep Suki in practice. Zeke was the only one to complain. As medical orderly, most of his supplies were being used to patch up the enthusiastic Russian.

Morelli ran the baseball instruction courses. The Russians enjoyed the sport. But it was Rhodes who was the dunce of Morelli's class. He'd stand on the diamond, holding his bat as though he were playing cricket at Lords, and complain of unsporting body-line bowling. Morelli was patient, but found it hard to overlook Rhodes's habit of running to first base, and back again, and claiming it as a run.

The hooch points became the Island's international currency. The Russians and Americans used them as money in their nightly card games and for gambling. The Russians found that the points for half a bottle of fruit-brandy would buy them a carton of American cigarettes. And Americans discovered that the points for half a dozen bottles of fruit-brandy could get them a camera or a pair of Soviet binoculars.

The still continued to turn out its quota of spirits. Twice the Americans sent out emergency radio calls for more fruit juice and vegetables. Corrigan claimed it was a precaution against scurvy. The aircraft flew in low over the Island and dropped the supplies. Again they fell neatly into the Russian sector. This time it made no difference.

The evenings were the best part of very pleasant days. Continual experiments by Ushakov were now producing a far superior drink. The addition of spices gave it a distinctive flavour which hid the mustiness. After dinner, the men would gather in groups on the trawler, on the plateau and in the American Mess. They talked, they joked, they sang and they drank. Often they gambled.

At sunset, three flags were lowered to the one bugle call. The Stars and Stripes at the western end of the Island. The Soviet flag from the trawler's mast on the eastern end of the Island. And, from a short flagmast between the two, Victoria and Tanya's contribution to the Island's new Government—a white cornucopia on an azure background.

The Prime Minister and the American President were talking once again on the Hot Line.

"The replacement cactus you sent? Oh, yes. It's doing very well. No, I don't need another. Thanks, anyway."

The trans-Atlantic line crackled as it died. The P.M. put down the receiver and walked over to the window of his office. The top of the cactus was level with his eyes. He leant out, carefully avoiding the spikes, and shouted to the gardener standing in the basement area thirty feet below.

"And while you're down there, throw a few gallons of water over the roots."

145

13

"Talk, you little bitch. Talk." There was a scuffle from behind the Mess. Then a loud shout.

"You bitch. Bite a Leatherneck, would ya? Now say Ah love you, or Ah'll stomp you to pulp." Zeke's angry voice startled Morelli and Hennessey who were on sunbathing duty on the parade ground.

"Christ," said Morelli. "What's Zeke up to. He's beating Vicky to death."

There was another shout.

"I'll stop him," said Hennessey. He leapt to his feet and ran, barefooted, round the back of the Mess.

Zeke was clutching a finger that dripped blood. He was standing, looking down into an old Coca-Cola crate.

"Say 'pretty boy'," he said coaxingly. There was silence from within the crate. "Talk," Zeke shouted. "Ya dumb bird."

Hennessey joined the tall Kentuckian and stared down into the strawlined box.

"A parrot," said Hennessey. "Where d'ya get it?"

"Found it sat by the sea," said Zeke. "It was covered in oil. Ah washed it. Kinda pretty, isn't it? Bites though."

Hennessey looked at the red and orange curved beak and decided not to take any close-range interest himself.

"Ah was going to teach it to talk, an' then give it to Vicky," said Zeke. "But it don't talk none."

"Maybe it's a slow learner."

"It could be Frenchee. 'Cus it don't understand pure American."

"Bon Jour," said Hennessey. The bird watched him sideways with one of its button eyes. It shuffled its orange legs. "Sure got funny feet for a parrot," he observed.

146

"How come?" said Zeke.

"It's got webs."

"Well, ain't some parrots got webbed feet?" asked Zeke.

"Only the swimming kind," said Hennessey. "And there ain't none."

"Maybe its pa was a duck. Hey, Major, sir," he called to Corrigan who was carrying out his camp inspection. Corrigan strode over.

"What you got there, Corporal?"

"Ah was just goin' to ask you, sir. Some sort of parrot."

Corrigan peered down into the crate.

"Where did you find that?"

"Down by the sea. Filthy with oil. Ah'm goin' to teach it to talk."

"Better if you taught it to swim again," said the Major. "It's a Puffin."

"Puffin?" asked Zeke.

"Yeah," said Corrigan. "A sort of seagull."

"MA-JOR . . ." Morelli swung himself round the corner of the Mess. "We got visitors. Look." He pointed out to sea. A small boat approached at high speed.

Corrigan ran to the plateau. "Call assembly," he bellowed.

The bugler half waded, half ran out of the sea, where he had been swimming. He dived into his tent for his bugle. He crawled out and blew assembly while he was still walking towards the parade ground on his knees. The men dropped everything. Russians and Americans came running.

Vorolokov panted over. "What's the matter?"

"Visitors. Get that barrier back. Make like we're nearly at war. That's how they'll expect to find us."

Vorolokov doubled to the trawler, shouting to his men as he ran.

"Get the gate closed," called Corrigan. "Get the rocket uncovered. Get yourselves dressed and collect your weapons. You," he pointed to Morelli. "On guard. Quick."

Corrigan hoped that nobody on board the approaching boat was using binouclars.

One by one the Marines crawled half-naked into tents. They stumbled out again, buttoning up denims, and fastening boots.

147

The cover was off the rocket launcher in seconds. "Aim it just above the trawler's bow, so you've got the bridge in your sights," shouted Ace. "Now get her loaded." The men dragged the rocket cases out and slid the missiles into the launcher. "Look like you're going to use it." The men crouched beside the weapon.

Ace called up to Vorolokov on the bridge. "How's it look?"

The Russian skipper gave him the thumbs up sign. "Fine," he shouted. "But don't press trigger."

"Morelli," shouted Hennessey. "Fasten yer flies. Try to look like a Marine. Get that cigarette outa your mouth."

"Zeke, hide the bottles in the Mess," reminded the Major. "This is a war zone. Make it look like action. Real action."

On the Russian side, the scarlet nose cone of the rocket arced out of the trawler's hull and hung threateningly thirty feet above the deck. Vorolokov clipped a machine-gun into place on the trawler's bow. On the watchtower beside the barrier, Sacha clambered up the ladder collecting the Marine's drying washing as he went. He rolled it into a ball and sat on it, while nursing his sub-machinegun. The fat Rasputin was dragged away from the trash can, and Lev resumed his old patrol along the frontier, hauling the dog behind him.

Mischa and Ace pushed the wire barrier back into place and chained it to the metal stakes driven into the rocks. "See you later, Mish," smiled Ace, looking at the Russian through the high fence.

The boat was flying the Stars and Stripes. It was now only fifty yards away from the Island.

"If we've forgotten anything," said Corrigan quietly to Ace, "it's too late now. Guards," he shouted. "Get down to the beach and help that boat."

'Suki, sir," called Morelli.

Corrigan looked in the direction of the Marine's pointing hand. The large Filipino was clambering down the rope ladder of the *Dmitri Kirov*. He saw the American boat approaching, and the sudden change in the Island, and climbed back up again.

Corrigan turned back towards the landing area. As he did so, he caught sight of a figure emerging from the latrines. "Holy Cow, Igor!" The Major almost panicked ."Hennessey," he shouted. "That man, improperly dressed," he waved wildly at the Cossack. "Get his name. Put him on report."

Hennessey's reactions were quick. He grabbed the startled Igor and frogmarched him to the cookhouse tent. "Get him a uniform, Zeke, and keep him outa the way."

The boat crunched onto the beach. Surrounded by armed American sailors sat a white-haired, grandfatherly figure, with a professional smile. "Hi," it called to Corrigan. "Come to see my boys."

"Oh, no," thought the Major. "Not the Alabama Fireball." But aloud, he greeted the visitor. "Good to see you again, Sir."

Senator Alvin Bernard Courtney Soupe, known in the Senate as Alphabet, leant on the arm of a young matelot and stepped over the side of the boat. He walked up the beach, his fat hand extended. A camera-carrying Naval Officer followed a few steps behind. The shutter clicked repeatedly as he recorded the front line visit for official release to the American Press.

Senator Soupe clasped Corrigan's hands with both of his own, then put his arm round the Major's shoulder.

"Gotta let you boys know the folks back home are thinking of you. You're doing a fine job. A handful of tough American boys facing the challenge to the Free World. We're proud of you. Show me around. I want to see everything. I want to meet everyone. You're no forgotten outpost. I'm gonna tell everyone about you when I get home."

"Happy to have you here, sir," said Corrigan. He remembered that back home it was election year.

"I hear you guys are having one hell of a tough time. How are the men taking it?"

"Always full of spirit, sir," said Corrigan, truthfully.

"What about the Reds?"

"I don't think they can take much more. We keep 'em bottled up."

"Great, great. This here the frontier?" the Senator asked superfluously, pointing at the wire. "And is that a Ruskie?"

On cue, Lev put on a fierce look. He jerked the fat Rasputin to his feet. The dog caught sight of Zeke standing in the background, and pulled at the leash. Lev barked.

"God, that's a man-eater if there ever was one," said Soupe.

"A real killer, sir. Attacked the Lieutenant in his tent one night. We dealt with it. There was a red trail back to the wire next morning. Hasn't troubled us since."

Corrigan winked across the barrier at Lev.

The clicking of the camera shutter became monotonous. It only stopped when the photographer changed spools. Morelli stood by the wire, his carbine unslung and at the ready. He was chewing slowly and was staring iron-faced across the frontier.

"Been on guard long, soldier?" asked Soupe.

"All night, sir. Something's brewing on the other side."

"Great. Great." Soupe turned to the photographer. "Shoot one of me with this man. I'm proud to know you, son," he told Morelli. Soupe grabbed the Marine's hand and postured for the photographer. He pulled in his stomach and puffed out his chest until it pulled at the lightweight fabric of his pale blue suit. The shutter clicked.

"Show me more," said Soupe. Corrigan led him to the parade ground, where Hennessey was working out a drill squad.

"Left, right, left, about turn. Left, right, left, about turn. Left, right, left, about turn," he bawled. The men covered three lengths of the diminutive parade ground in nine paces. "Halt. Right face." As Hennessey saw the VIP arrive, he shouted: "Present arms." There was a smart slap as the men obeyed.

Soupe was impressed. "Great. Great. Never seen better."

"Thank you, sir," said Corrigan.

"What's the orange tent," asked Soupe.

"They're the British," said Corrigan briefly. "Security. They're not allowed off. We don't see much of them. They stay in the tent most of the time. They claim it's a sort of Embassy." He hoped as he said this that Rhodes would keep out of sight. The Major knew that the solicitor and Collins had drunk too much breakfast.

Corrigan tried to steer the Senator into the Mess, but Soupe wanted a full tour. He examined the rocket launcher. He visited every latrine. He tugged at the chains in all the showers, and he crawled in and out of the pup tents. The

150

camera kept clicking. He admired the PX store, where Corrigan just had time to slip a pair of Russian binoculars behind a counter. Then he strode purposely towards the cook-tent.

With a shiver, Corrigan remembered Igor. He tried once more to lead Soupe into the Mess. Again he failed.

"I want to see the cook," said Soupe, nodding in the direction of the cookhouse.

"I'll call him out," the Major offered hopefully.

"Nope. Don't want to disturb a man at his work." Soupe went in.

Igor was sitting on a stool at the far end, with his head down. He was peeling his way through a tottering pyramid of potatoes—with a machete. He selected a potato, held it on the chopping block, and with six deft strokes cut it into a tidy cube. The extra-thick peel he carefully washed and put neatly into the still's fermentation drum at his side. The squared potatoes, which he knew were only to be used for eating, he built into a childlike fortification around him.

The Cossack was wearing one of the tall Kentucky cook's ample combat suits. Zeke's steel helmet almost rested on Igor's shoulders. He could have taken his feet out of the boots without unlacing them.

Zeke stepped in front of the strange figure, and tried to hide it.

"You the cook?" asked Soupe.

"Yes, sir."

"Where you from, son?" Soupe looked up at him.

"Kentucky, sir."

He gave Zeke a playful punch in the ribs. "D'you make moonshine, son?" he joked. Zeke gulped.

"Nothing else but, sir."

"That's my Southern boys. Greatest sense of humour in the United States," he said to Corrigan. The Major smiled sickly.

"Who's he?" Soupe pointed at Igor, dwarfed behind his growing castellated wall.

"Him? Oh, him." Corrigan thought quickly. He tried to think of a name, but couldn't. "He's Corrigan," said Corrigan.

"But that's your name," said Soupe.

"Yeah." Corrigan's brain was a tangled confusion. He never panicked in battle. But here, in a cookhouse tent, he did. "He, he's ... He's my aunt ... er ... my aunt's son ... er ... my cousin, sir." The Major looked relieved.

"Ah, no favouritism here," noted Soupe. "Fine democratic unit you run, Major. Come over here boy." He beckoned to Igor.

"What's your first name, son?"

"Igor," said Igor.

"That's an unusual name?"

Igor looked cross. "Many peoples round Mozdok is named Igor."

"Mozdok?"

"Yes, sir," interrupted Corrigan. "Mozdok, New Jersey."

"Some of you Yankees have strange accents," said Soupe.

Corrigan touched the Senator's sleeve and jerked his head in the direction of the door. Soupe followed him out.

"I'm sorry, sir," he said confidentially. "He's our only casualty. He's suffering from battle fatigue. He volunteered for everything and drove himself into the ground. He's getting his speech back now. He's a brave kid."

"He looks very thin," said Soupe with concern.

"Yes," said Corrigan. "You know, he filled that uniform when he first arrived. He won't eat. We think it's occupational therapy for him to work in the cookhouse. Zeke looks after him."

"I'll get him a medal." Soupe's eyes blazed with patriotism.

"No, don't do that," said Corrigan hastily. "You'll ruin everything. I mean, a medal will remind him of the ordeal. It might set back his treatment."

"I'll take him out with me then," said Soupe. "The President will want to meet him. I'll get him on television. I'll make him a national hero. I'll get him the best medical treatment there is. I'd be proud to have a son like him."

Corrigan was appalled. Mentally, he pictured the devastation Igor could cause in the United States. He could imagine Igor meeting the President; Igor being interviewed on coast-to-coast television; Igor addressing the United Nations; Igor attending society balls. And Igor dancing ... on tables. Corrigan had to stop. The thoughts made his stomach freeze.

152

He tried to think of a way to stop Soupe's enthusiasm. He couldn't.

"Believe me, sir. I think he'd be better here with his friends. We'll nurse him. We need him. He'll be fighting fit in no time."

"No, I insist. Just think what this boy's sacrifices will do for morale back home." The Senator was sobbing with emotion.

Corrigan thought urgently.

"Senator, he's my cousin. Please let me handle it my way."

Senator Soupe saw Igor as his passport to re-election. He countered every argument that Corrigan put up.

"But Major, can't you see what this would do for the Marine Corps?"

"Only too well, Senator."

"Then why don't you let me ask the boy whether he wants to come with me?" Before Corrigan could reply, the Senator shouted, "Igor. Igor Corrigan."

Igor stumbled into the open.

"Here, son," said the Senator, gently, "how would you like to come to the United States with me?"

Delight flooded Igor's eyes. "Da," he said. "Much very."

"Now, hear that, Major. He called me Dad."

Corrigan was stunned at this development. He visualised himself on the parade ground, his epaulettes and buttons being torn off, and his sword being broken over his head in the traditional manner. Eternal disgrace would grip his military family. His father, a colonel, would be ostracised from his bridge club.

Soupe burst into Corrigan's unhappy thoughts.

"I must have a picture with this boy by the barrier." He took Igor's arm and walked him slowly over to the wire. Zeke watched, open-mouthed, from the cookhouse door. He could see ignominy heaped on the whole unit. It was going to be either them or Igor, he thought.

Soupe turned to his photographer. "Try to get that big cruel-looking Russian in the background," he said. He nodded his head at Suki, who, dressed in a blue boilersuit, now stood by Lev on the Russian side of the frontier. Suki

153

was absent-mindedly cocking and uncocking a Russian sub-machinegun he held under his arm.

The shutter clicked again.

"One more," said the photographer. Igor beamed.

"Gees," said Soupe to the defeated Major. "They ought to pay you guys double to have to look at such a mean and ugly monkey as that one." He pointed through the wire at US Marine Suki, who leered back.

Major Corrigan stared dumbly at the Filipino. "That one's a born trouble-maker," he said loudly. "Look at his eyes. They're too close together. If I had him over here, I'd soon knock that grin off his face."

Zeke called Igor into the cookhouse. There was just one chance that might save them all, he thought. "You want to please that man, Igor?"

"Da."

"When he speaks to you next time, just say to him 'All Johnny Rebs are goddammed sons-o'-bitches'. Got that?"

Igor rehearsed his lines. "Fine," said Zeke, crossing his fingers.

Igor walked back to join the Senator and Corrigan at the frontier. The Kentucky cook looked up at the ceiling of the tent. "Gran'pappy Hatfield, please forgive me for blasphemin' your memory," he whispered. Then he stood and listened.

He didn't have to wait long. There was a sudden explosive oath from the visiting dignitary.

"Sergeant Hennessey," shouted Corrigan. Hennessey ran to the Major's side. "Arrest this Marine," blazed Corrigan, pointing at the still-smiling Igor. "Take him away. Lock him up. Get him out of sight. I don't want to see him again for thirty days."

Hennessey dragged the startled Cossack behind the orange tent.

"Aren't you being a bit too hard?" asked Soupe. "Maybe it's his battle fatigue."

Corrigan wasn't going to let this opportunity escape.

"He's like this all the time," he said. "I tried to warn you. He hates Southerners. Insults them at every chance. Thoroughly unpredictable character. His mother was frightened by *Gone With The Wind* when she was pregnant. He wasn't my choice as cousin."

"Pity," said Soupe. "I could have done a lot for him." He thought of his fickle electors.

The Senator's duty tour of inspection was over. He refused lunch. "Haven't time. Got to get back to the fleet." He was suddenly in a hurry. "I'll have a sandwich," he said to Zeke. "I'll try to get you boys some entertainment," he told the Marines, gathering on the shore to see him off.

Zeke brought him the sandwich. The Senator took it and walked down to his boat. He climbed aboard. As it pulled away he waved the sandwich at Corrigan. "Great, great," he called. "You're doing a fine job, boys."

There was a sudden hiss of air and a yelp from the Senator. Cedric, the lame seagull, swished down out of the sky and neatly extracted the ham protruding from the sandwich, leaving Soupe holding the empty bread. His comments were lost in the noise of the boat's engine.

Corrigan turned to Zeke.

"Thanks for the help with Igor, Zeke. You did us all a big favour. Put up an extra stripe. You just made sergeant."

Zeke smiled. The insult to gran'pappy's memory had been erased.

It was draughty in the chandeliered Throne Room of the antique Royal Palace. The Queen pulled her ermine-fringed robe even closer and shuddered. The Prime Minister was speaking.

He gazed out at her from the screen of a six-inch, battery-powered Japanese television set. He was having difficulty in deciding which camera he should be addressing perfectly frankly and honestly at that particular moment.

"My children," he began, then corrected himself. "Fellow earthmen, er, Englishmen ... and people. Er, you have no doubt heard, er ..."—he scratched his forehead with the muzzle of his pipe, leaving a dark stain like a third eyebrow — —"... about the death of my cacti ... er, I mean, the troubles at Foul Rock. The Russians, er, and even the Americans, are completely responsible ..."

He paused. "All eleven of them died after shaving ... a

155

catastrophy . . . I blame thirteen years of opposition misrule . . . the Esso tiger . . . hippies . . . and bingo . . .'

The remainder of his nationwide speech tapered into silence as a sturdy corgi dog picked up the television set by its handle and carried it out of the room.

"Where's he gone?" Queen asked her husband.

"Only to the garden. He always buries the set when the P.M. speaks."

"We really ought to do something about him."

"Yes," replied Queen's husband. "I think he should be stuffed and donated to the Natural History Museum."

"Silly boy," chided Queen, affectionately. "I meant the Prime Minister."

"So did I," replied her husband.

14

Radio communication between the Islanders and the outside world was minimal. Days passed with the transceiver lying silent in Clancy Paradise's pup tent. At the moment it was buzzing wildly.

Clancy was lying on his stomach at the side of a clear rock pool, watching his winkle. It was a beaut. It was the biggest winkle, he hoped, in the world. It was just winning him eighty-five hooch points in the winkle sweepstake. Victoria had voted it Winkle of the Week. It outweighed Hennessey's black monster by all of a gramme.

Winkling was a morning pastime. The small sea snails the men found on the wet rocks were much prized by the GI and Russian fishermen for bait, and by the British as a tea-time delicacy. The men tried racing them without success. Although carefully painted in international car-racing colours, the winkles refused to co-operate. They were content to rest motionless for hours in a rock pool. So, instead, the men gambled on their size. The biggest winkle found each week took the sweepstake. This was always hard on the winning winkle—it was part of the rules that it should be eaten before nightfall. Clancy's winkle was now doomed.

Clancy was sad. He'd found this one on Monday, and had nurtured it for five days. His feelings towards the shellfish were quite fatherly. He gentled it with his finger. It pulled its coiled house down until just the tip of the black body was visible. Clancy imagined it smiling to itself in the darkness.

"Here's your hooch points," said Ace. "And there's the cookpot."

The winning winkle always had the honour of being the first one into the boiling water. This way there was no

157

possibility of cheating. The same winkle could never win twice. The losing gamblers would stand around and watch the ceremony. Then they would drop their own sea snails into the excited pan, or the bait tins.

Clancy picked up the winkle between his thumb and forefinger. The snail pulled back into its shell and shut the small horn door, as it sought the safety of its home.

"I don't want to win," said Clancy gruffly. "I'm going to keep the winkle."

"What do you mean?" asked Ace. "There's eighty-five hooch points here. You've won, so take your winnings."

"Give them to Hennessey."

Clancy carried the winkle carefully down to the sea. He waded in until the water reached his armpits. The astounded Russian and American gamblers watched him draw back his arm and throw the winning winkle far out. Then he turned and waded ashore.

"I couldn't do it," he apologised. "It's all right when they're strangers, but I got to know that one."

The crackling of the radio saved him from further embarrassment. He crawled into the tent and clamped the headset over his red face.

"Call the Major," he shouted through the doorway.

"Mail, supplies and a special delivery," called Corrigan to the men. "Eager Mary says there's a landing craft on the way."

There was a cheer from the Marines. This was the first mail since their arrival on the Island. Supplies were always welcome.

"Get over and warn Usha that we're going to have more visitors," Corrigan told Ace. "At least we've got a bit of warning this time. And tell him to put Igor in chains until the ship leaves."

Getting the Island prepared for visitors was easy this time. There was no rush, and the men had benefited from the panic of the previous week. This time, Corrigan held a roll call. Everyone was present.

"Right," he said. "Stay put. Sergeant Hennessey, check every tent and hut and make sure Igor isn't in our half. I couldn't go through that again."

Everything was orderly and suitably warlike by the time the landing craft beached itself on the Island. It was manned by Grunts from the men's own Company back with the Fleet.

"What's it like here, Morelli?" shouted one of the men.

"Man, it's number ten. We never know when we might get action. Ain't nobody lending money around here."

"See that ship," Suki joined in the shouted conversation. He pointed at the trawler. "And that big rocket. It's a baby nuke. A Red pokes the button and it goes up twenty miles. Then it comes down. Right about here."

"Jesus," said the visiting Grunt, tossing Suki a mailbag.

"Bet you got nothin' to do all day, 'cept sit on yer fat butts in the sun," said a blue-chinned Marine.

"Twenty-four-hour guards, weapon training, three drill parades a day, kit inspections every morning, lousy grub, fish till we're sick of it, never more than fifty yards from an officer. Brother, I'll change with you, any time," replied Clancy.

"It's a nerve war," added Morelli. "Them Reds never let up. Try being followed by a gunsight everywhere you go. Ain't relaxing."

"Darlings," said a voice from the landing craft.

"Funny," said Suki to Hennessey. "Draft Board must be getting careless."

"Darlings," said the voice again. "Darlings, give me a hand with my baggage."

"Did you jus' hear what I heard?" Hennessey asked Suki.

"He ain't sharing my tent," said the Filipino.

"Be a sweetie," called the voice again. "Carry me ashore and I'll give you a kiss."

"Cut the comedy, Marine," shouted Hennessey angrily. "This is a war zone. Carry your own baggage." He turned to the men on the beach. "Get those supplies unloaded, fast."

An oddly-shaped Marine staggered from the landing craft, weighted down with suitcases. Corrigan stared. It was a strange build for a Grunt, he thought, but a classic shape for a woman. It was a woman! What threw him was he'd never before seen a 36-23-36 inch combat suit on a 38-23-36 figure . . . a female's at that! She overflowed. The front buttons of her tunic were undone almost to the waist. The

159

buttons that remained fastened pulled at the material. Her red lace bra, structurally inadequate, barely coped with its task.

"Blast!" She dropped her suitcases, stumbled and sat down heavily on top of one of them, examining a broken fingernail.

"Freeeeze . . ." shouted Corrigan, as there was a stampede towards her. His commanding voice penetrated the tattoo of combat boots on the rocks. The men stopped, frozen in a collection of exaggeratedly ridiculous poses. Corrigan picked his way through the khaki statues.

As he stopped in front of her, she shook her long copper hair back off her face and looked up. Her eyes were like green traffic lights. Her flickering eyelashes signalled "go-ahead". She smiled. The Major proceeded with caution.

"I'm Dreamy."

"Ye-es," said Corrigan.

"Dreamy Knights."

There were groans of ecstasy from the statues.

"I'm a performer," she breathed.

"I'll bet," said a dozen voices.

"Get on with the unloading," Corrigan ordered.

"If you're Major Corrigan, I've got a letter for you," said the featherbed voice. It was so soft he was glad he had to bend closer to hear it. "I'm up here," continued the voice.

Corrigan dragged his eyes back. She handed him an envelope. It was a note from Senator Soupe. Scribbled calculatedly on the back of an electioneering pamphlet. It read: "Promised I wouldn't forget the boys. Thanks for your hospitality. Nothing's too good for you. I asked them to send you Bob Hope."

Corrigan looked up. Her perfume engulfed him. He was drowning.

"Sorry," said Dreamy. "Bob had to go on a Far East tour. You've got to have me."

"I have?" asked Corrigan. "I mean, glad you're with us."

The landing craft was backing off the beach. The Marines shouted their goodbyes. "Hope we see you again," called a sad-faced Grunt on its bow.

"Bring us a package like this every time you come," replied Morelli.

Corrigan led the girl up to the Mess. There was no shortage of porters for her luggage.

"What she do?" asked Hennessey.

Dreamy turned her green eyes on the men. She wiggled her hips. "I sing and dance, Sergeant."

"Woweeeee," shouted the Marines.

"Are you staying long?" asked Corrigan.

"As long as you need me," breathed Dreamy.

By mutual and unspoken assent it was decided it would be safest not to tell the new arrival the true situation on the Island for the time being. The guards were relaxed but the men stayed in their uniforms, and on their own sides of the wire for the rest of the day.

It wasn't easy finding accommodation for the guest. Victoria made the generous sacrifice. She moved Albert out of his compartment. He accepted Igor and Sacha's offer to share their cabin on the *Dmitri Kirov*.

Morelli spent a couple of hours polishing and cleaning the Mess piano. Many of the higher notes were dead, and some of the ivory had lifted off the keys, but it seemed to be almost in tune.

The tone-deaf Hennessey tested it. "Perfect," he proclaimed.

For the first time in weeks, only the Americans and British ate dinner together in the Mess. Zeke had carefully made sure that there were only twenty-two chairs around the two long tables.

"Sing for us," asked Clancy when the last plates had been passed back to the cookhouse. "Sing us some love songs."

Dreamy moved across to the piano. Morelli switched off the main lights in the Mess. Only one, hanging directly above the piano, was left on. Fitted with an aluminium foil cover, it lit Dreamy like a spotlight. Smoke from the men's cigarettes drifted through its beam. Dreamy sang. The men were quiet. The applause seemed to grow louder after each number. An hour later, she turned round to her audience.

"Sorry boys, that's your quota for tonight."

"Aw, come on Dreamy."

161

L

"If you want me to have a voice tomorrow, you'll have to let me rest it now."

The room was now thick with smoke. Morelli switched on the lights. Dreamy was startled. When the room had been darkened there had been an audience of only twenty-one. Now the audience seemed to have doubled. Men she didn't recognise clapped her as she stood up. Strange men, wearing thick sweaters and black uniforms, bowed to her as she walked back to her table. And there was another girl, whom she hadn't seen before, standing by the door, smiling at her.

"Who are they?" she asked Victoria.

"I'll tell you later."

Corrigan saw her looking around and attracted her attention with a question. "Where did you work before?"

"Around," said Dreamy. "Around most places. Vaudeville, cabaret, night clubs. I like night clubs best of all."

"Night clubs," said Ace. "I haven't been in one since my last home furlough. Sure wish I could walk into the Orchid Room right now."

"Last time Morelli was in one, he was a sergeant," said Suki.

"Knock it off, Suki. I know how to behave in a night club, like anyone else."

"Not like anyone else I know."

"I have not been in a night club for twenty-five years," said a bearded face. "We do not have many in Russia."

Dreamy stared at him.

Corrigan interrupted fiercely. "It's way past Taps," he said. "Better hit the sack." He took Dreamy by the arm. "I'll see you and Vicky back to the tent."

"If he didn't have the rank . . ." grumbled a voice.

Corrigan had been worried about having to explain the situation to Dreamy. He needn't have been. She accepted it almost without comment. It meant more of an audience. It meant more men.

When she pegged out her washing, the morning after her arrival, it was almost a cabaret in itself. She couldn't have worn all the clothes that she hung out. And she wouldn't have carried them around dirty. Black frilly briefs. Blue mini

162

briefs. Crimson lace panties. The red bra they'd all seen, and several others that the men hoped to see again — filled.

At first the men tried to avoid being caught looking at the line. It was impossible. It attracted their eyes like the headlamps of an oncoming car at night.

Victoria's washing, which had previously seemed interesting, was now dull. Tanya's was matronly by comparison.

The three girls were inside the tent. The only sight the men had caught of Dreamy was during the brief moments she was hanging out her cabaret.

Albert looked at the bright line of underwear, fluttering a sensuous message in the warm breeze.

"Nelson hung out a signal like that on the day of the battle of Trafalgar," he said.

"Yeah?"

"Yep. It said, 'England expects every man this day to do his duty.'"

"What happened?"

"He got killed," said Albert.

"In the rush?" asked Morelli.

"I don't reckon they should send pretty girls out to entertain the troops," said Clancy. "They should send knotty old broads." The rest of the men looked at him incredulously.

"Sure," he went on. "Dishy broads is an aphrodisiac. My John Thomas thinks I've taken Holy Orders." He turned to Suki. "You're the keep-fit man round here, what happens when you don't use a muscle?"

"It shrivels away."

"Oh," said Clancy, unhappily. "I thought it was the cold water."

"Don't you like women, Gin Jim?" Clancy asked Rhodes, who was sitting in his deckchair in the sun.

"I've known a few. But no man's got room for more than three vices. I've got Gordon's gin, Booth's gin, and Plymouth gin."

The flagmast shuddered as Suki shrugged himself upright among the men. He was reading a long white form which had arrived for him with the mail.

"It says here, any athletic feats. What's it mean?"

Hennessey looked up at him, puzzled.

"It's a misprint. Must be. Oughta read, any athlete's foot? You know, foot rot. Tell 'em no, you ain't got foot rot."

"Why should they want to know if I got foot rot?" asked Suki.

"Well, it's a health resort, ain't it? They wouldn't want a rash of foot rot with all them wealthy clients, would they? Why d'ya want to work there, anyhows? Why don't you get diving work. It pays better. Why don't you sign for another stretch. You'd make sergeant." Hennessey didn't like the idea of his friend considering leaving the Corps.

"I've already done twelve years. It's time I changed my career. Think of the rich dames in a health resort. I'd be teaching them calesthenics. An' I get food and keep, free. And a uniform."

"A uniform and free food—that's a change?" asked Hennessey.

Suki looked around for someone who was likely to give him more support than his friend.

"Excuse me, Ace, sir." He stopped the young Lieutenant who was walking towards the Mess. "Will you give me a hand, sir? I'm trying to fill in an application for a job."

"Going to leave us, then?" asked Ace. "Thought you were a regular."

"I am, sir. At least, I finish my hitch in another couple of months. Thought I'd write for a job as an instructor in a health resort. Trouble is, they didn't tell me I'd have to be a clerk as well. I've never been good at filling in forms."

"Give it here,' said Ace. "I'll fill it in from your records. All you'll have to do then is to sign it." He took the form, folded it, and poked it into the front of his swim shorts.

Corrigan called over from the door of his tent.

"Right, men. Lobster patrol. What's keeping you?"

There was an unwilling movement towards the boat. The flap of the orange tent was drawn back and Dreamy stepped out.

"Who's Morelli?" she called.

The Marines stopped, and looked back.

"Can you come here?" she asked.

"Fasten your flies," hissed Ace, automatically.

"I'm in a swimsuit, sir." Morelli blushed, and pushed his

164

way through the men towards the tent. Dreamy took him by the arm and confidentially whispered something in his ear. They went inside.

"She's starting with the ugly ones first," said Suki.

Morelli's head reappeared. "Better go without me. I'm busy."

"How come she wants you, Macaroni?"

"She's heard about me." His head disappeared. There were groans from the Marines.

They didn't see much of Morelli all day. Every time they spotted him, he was always with Boris, or with one of the girls. He scuttled off without answering their questions. He dodged the day's duties.

The men found that now there was a new form of entertainment to look forward to in the evening, the day seemed longer. Dreamy's presence gave them a sense of frustration that they hadn't felt before. Unlike the two other girls, she belonged to the Grunts . . . well, almost.

It was a relief when Zeke shouted them into dinner. The Americans and Russians lined up at Mess.

"Zeke, where's all the chairs an' tables gone?" asked Clancy Paradise.

"What chairs and tables?"

"Our chairs an' tables, you Kentucky beanstalk."

The men looked around them. The Mess was almost empty of furniture. Even the piano was missing.

"How we goin't to eat?" asked Clancy.

"Eat on the rocks," said Zeke. "Tonight, men, you got a new dish. Chicken Maryland on the Rocks." He laughed, alone.

"Jeez," said Hennessey. "This place is gettin' to be a dump. Just like home."

"Here, Suki. Sign this. It's all filled in for you."

Ace Ellsmore handed the Filipino a pen and a folded form. Suki scrawled his name on the dotted line. "I'll send it off for you," said Ace, taking back the paper. "It'll go in the next mail collection. By the way, where's Dreamy?"

"I'd rather know where Victoria is," said Albert. "I haven't seen her all day." He looked round the group of men as though he was trying to decide who also was missing.

"Maybe they're ALL sharing Morelli."

"Yeah," said Suki. "Where's Ravioli, anyway? He ain't missed a meal in his entire service."

"Tanya's been very busy, too," said Vorolokov, balancing his food tray on his knees, and tearing a strip of meat off the chicken leg.

"Much goings about," said Igor. "Everybody not here. Boris also. I not see Mischa."

"I thought we was going to get entertainment with our meals," said Hennessey.

"Ain't Zeke's cookin' funny enough for you?" asked Suki.

" 'Ello," interrupted Albert. "Here's Victoria. She's in a bit of a state."

Victoria was swinging down the rope ladder from the trawler's deck. She dropped the last few feet and walked over to the men. She had a smug look. Her clothes were dusty and her face was streaked with perspiration and dirt. Her hair was tied back and covered with a scarf.

"You have been shining my ship?" asked Vorolokov.

"No, we've been fixing up your Mess for Dreamy. She wants to give a show tonight."

"Great," said Ace. "What time?"

"Any time after eight." She hurried back towards the trawler.

"What about your dinner?" called Zeke. He didn't get an answer.

Victoria had said eight o'clock and the Marines and Russians were determined not to miss a minute of the promised treat. By a quarter to eight, all the Island's male inhabitants were standing expectantly on the deck of the *Dmitri Kirov*. Morelli was guarding the top of the companionway leading down to the Mess.

"Can't we go in and wait, Morelli?" asked Ace.

"Sorry, sir, got my orders."

"Let us in, you jerk," said Suki.

"Piss off," said Morelli, firmly.

The men waited impatiently, lounging against the rail of the ship, or standing around the self-important Morelli. They grumbled. At exactly eight o'clock, they heard Tanya's voice.

166

"Open now," she called.

Morelli was carried backwards by the Niagara of men rushing down the ladder towards the invitation. The Russians had the advantage. They knew exactly where to go. Some of the Marines who had not regularly visited the ship found themselves rushing into cabins or fire hose lockers. Eventually the men found themselves in a compacted group at the Mess door. Igor and the other Russian seamen were trying to read a large white notice pinned to the woodwork.

"Dreamy's Dive Bar," it said. "Members only."

"What it speaking?" asked Igor.

"It says you got to be a member," said Suki.

"What is member?"

"You've got to have a card."

"I got card," said Igor, proudly.

"You have?"

Igor felt in his pocket and pulled out his wallet. He opened it. "Look," he said. "Seaman Union card."

"Try knocking," called Ace over the heads of the men.

Suki knocked. The men waited anxiously. After a moment the door opened a few inches.

"Who there?" asked Tanya, fatuously.

"Batman and Robin. Let us in."

"Very funniness," said Tanya. "Entrance slowly."

She opened the door wider. The men walked in. It was so dark inside that it took them a little while to get accustomed to the gloom.

"Great heavens," said Corrigan.

"Impossible." Vorolokov stared.

The Mess no longer resembled the trawler's canteen. The walls and deckhead were draped with fishing nets and life-belts. A couple of small anchors were crossed as the central decoration on the side walls. The American and Soviet flags hung side by side on the end wall. The main light was covered by a deep orange shade, made from one of the plastic marker floats. It cast a warm glow over a miniature dance floor surrounded by tables, their scrubbed tops hidden under signal flags. On them stood bottles with yellow ship's candles stuck in their necks. The small flames were sucked and buffeted by the draught from the door.

The cosy, intimate atmosphere of the previously austere

167

Mess was surprising. But even more astonishing were the outfits worn by Tanya and Victoria. They were both dressed alike in black tights from Dreamy's wardrobe. They wore close fitting white seamen's sweaters, borrowed from the Russian bosun's stores, belted at the waist so that they looked like the miniest of brief dresses. Both had their hair piled high and silver foil coronets glistened as they moved.

Mischa sat beside the piano, in one corner. He played his balalaika softly as the men entered. They were almost too stunned to talk as Victoria and Tanya showed them to their tables and took their orders for hooch. It was like a dream.

"Great," said Ace, looking around. "Just great." He watched Victoria walk past, her long legs even more attractive in the stagey tights.

The men relaxed, the noise increased. Mischa boosted the volume and tempo of his music. The smoke from the men's cigarettes hung in layers. They drank. The atmosphere was complete. By the time most had finished their second glass of hooch, the men felt they had been in the club all evening. Mischa sang. The men joined in.

The music stopped. At exactly the right moment Dreamy made her entrance. The men cheered. She swept into the light. She dazzled them. Thousands of sequins on her ankle length dress twinkled. The backless gown, cut well below her waist, had only a little more material at the front. It plunged widely between her breasts almost to her navel. She curtseyed. Then she sang.

Dreamy's repartee with her audience was slick and practised. Between songs, she flirted with the men. Every Russian and American wanted her. She was an expert. When she called for the men to sing with her, they sang. When she demanded silence, they scarcely breathed. When she finished, they cheered. Dreamy stepped over to Corrigan and pulled him up onto the small dance floor. The men cheered again. She pulled Corrigan close to her and smooched with him to Mischa's music. For that moment, the Major was the most envied man on the Island.

"Come on," said Victoria to Albert. They were joined by Tanya and Vorolokov. The girls were scrupulously fair. No man was allowed to dance with them for more than a few minutes. There were no wallflowers.

"And now," called Dreamy, when at last Mischa's music stopped. "We offer you the facilities of the casino section of the Club. Honest Luigi Morelli, Head Croupier of Dreamy's Dive Bar, invites you to join him at the roulette table." She waved to one side of the room.

Morelli stood behind a long table where a sheet of white paper had been marked off in numbered squares. In the centre of the table was a circular disc balanced, like a cymbal, on a spike driven into a block of wood. On the disc was painted a pointer. When spun, the arrow came to rest opposite numbers painted on a dial on the white paper beneath.

"Place ya bets, gentlemen," called Morelli. The men wandered over. Soon there was a crowd standing around the table. It might have been unorthodox, but it was gambling, and it was square. Hooch points changed hands.

"How about that? I won," said Suki as he and Hennessey made their way back to their table. "Must be my lucky day."

"Luckier than you'll ever know," said Hennessey.

"What you mean?" asked Suki. sharply.

"We saved you from bein' a gigolo."

"What gigolo?"

"We saved you from working on that health farm."

"How d'ya save me? I didn't want to be saved. I signed the paper."

"You signed a re-enlistment form, Buddy. Don't tell me you don't know one when you see it? You're in for another stretch." Hennessey smiled.

"You black pirate," yelled Suki. "You shanghaied me. You and that skinny Lieutenant."

"We jus' couldn't face the future without you." Hennessey was laughing. Suki grinned and then laughed with him. He punched Hennessey in the chest. The two men danced like shaggy bears on the dance floor.

"Let's get drunk," said Suki.

Dreamy's club was a great success. Drinking, singing, gambling and dancing. The men refused to allow Tanya and Victoria to wait at tables. They were too much in demand as dancing partners. They seldom sat down for more than a few seconds. It was impossible for them to refuse to dance. Dreamy moved from one partner to another.

Russian or American, it made no difference. She wriggled herself against them, ruffled their hair, whispered in their ears. They grinned, looked intoxicated and argued good humouredly when their dance was finished.

"Come dance with me, again," said Tanya to Vorolokov. She reached down and pulled him to his feet. He gulped the drink he was holding and put the cup down on the table.

"I am not good at dancing."

"Dance," insisted Tanya.

She took hold of his hands and pushed them around her, then she put both her arms round his neck. "Do you like our club?" she asked.

"You must have worked very hard today."

"All day. I worked to please you especially, as you said you had not been to a night club for twenty-five years."

"It wasn't such a good club as this," said Vorolokov.

"Do you like my dress?"

Vorolokov didn't answer for a moment. It was hard for him to explain. He was jealous that the other men could experience as much pleasure as he did in looking at this young girl.

"I like it," he said at last.

"I was afraid you might be angry," said Tanya. "I'm too hot in here. Will you come on deck with me for a few minutes?"

They danced their way around the small floor until they were opposite the door. Vorolokov led her out. They climbed the companionway and walked for'ard to the bow of the trawler.

"It's cool out here," said Tanya.

"This is a good place."

From below them they could hear the half-shouted conversations, laughter and music from the Mess.

"How long have you known me?" asked Tanya. She looked ahead of her over the American camp, towards the smooth sea beyond.

"Almost two years."

"And how long have I had a fiancé?"

"I didn't know that you had."

"I haven't. I haven't been out with a man in all that time."

170

"No?" said Vorolokov. He wondered what this was leading to.

"You are an old fool."

"I am an old fool," repeated Vorolokov.

"Must I do the asking?"

"What asking?"

"For two years I haven't been out with a man and you haven't wondered why. Do you think I'm a lesbian?" she asked.

"Of course not. I thought you were interested in your work."

"Vorolokov," said Tanya firmly. "Captain Vorolokov. I have a request to make."

"Make it," said Vorolokov.

"I request that you marry me."

Vorolokov was speechless. Tanya turned until she was looking up at him. "I would like an answer, my Captain."

"Have you thought about this? You are very young, and I am old."

"I am not very young. You are not very old."

He drew her towards him and touched her soft cheek with his work-roughened hand.

"Are you quite certain?"

"Yes."

"Then I grant you your request."

"I have another request, Captain."

"What is it this time?"

"Will you kiss me?"

When they returned to the night club half an hour later, it was like walking into a Montmartre cellar. Zeke's harmonica and Mischa's piano-playing had a distinctly Parisian sound. Dreamy lounged against a corner of the piano, her cigarette in a long ebony holder, husking a Left Bank ballad. They stood at the entrance and listened.

As usual, when Dreamy was singing, the chatter at the gaming table stopped. Morelli refused to take bets while she sang. Tanya waited until the song was over, and the men's cheering had died away. Then she clapped her hands, and walked into the centre of the room. Too late, Vorolokov realised what was about to happen.

171

"Comrades," she said. She looked happy and flushed. "I have a news to give. Captain Vorolokov is asking to make me his mistress."

There were cheers from the Americans.

Blushing apoplectically, Vorolokov pushed his way to Tanya's side, put his arm round her, and announced firmly: "Tonight, I have asked Tanya Suvorova to be my wife." He repeated it in Russian.

This time there were cheers from both sides.

Victoria and Dreamy ran forward and kissed Tanya on the cheeks. It was too good an opportunity for the men to miss. They crowded around, kissing Tanya, kissing Dreamy, kissing Victoria. The Russians even kissed Vorolokov. Not the Americans—they just shook his hand.

Vorolokov was dazed. He couldn't believe what had happened.

"Vodka," demanded Ushakov. Then he remembered. "Hooch," he corrected. "We drink a toast to their happiness."

"I say toast," cried Igor, waving his beaker in the air.

"Please, no," pleaded Boris. "It is too much expensive. We have these cups only."

Corrigan rose to his feet. He held his cup high. "To the Captain and his mate," he roared. Everyone drank.

Victoria glanced at her father, who had been sitting with Albert and Collins in a corner. Three dead bottles stood on the table. She could see he had a speech coming on. He was straightening his wig, and fixing an important look on his face. Before he had time to take the next step, which was clearing his throat, she grabbed a bottle from Zeke's table and topped up her father's glass. The thoughts of a speech disappeared down his throat with the drink.

Earlier, the men drank because it seemed to be the thing to do in the club. Now they felt they had a genuine cause for a celebration. Hooch points were forgotten and the fruit-brandy stock was taking a beating. It was comforting to Rhodes to know that even while they drank, the still was quietly dribbling its daily quota into the bottles.

"I dance," shouted Igor.

"We dance," corrected Suki. He and Hennessey joined the young Cossack on the floor. Mischa first played a slow tune. The dance that the three men concocted wasn't exactly Cossack. It wasn't exactly a dance. It was a small riot set to music. It attracted the others. Normally, none of the Russians would have competed directly with Igor, but now they joined in. The Americans followed them out of high spirits. The room thudded as the men tried to copy Igor.

Hennessey, supported on either side by Suki and Morelli, imitated the Russians' high kicking. Igor shouted the movements like the caller at a hoe-down. Vorolokov and Ushakov urged Corrigan on. Mischa was enjoying himself. Tears of laughter ran down his creased face as he watched the dancers. He was gradually increasing the tempo. The end was inevitable. Someone tripped. The next second there were a dozen bodies sprawled on top of each other in a laughing heap on the floor.

"Now you dance for us, Dreamy," shouted Zeke.

"Yes. Da. Dreamy dance for us," chorused the men. "Dreamy dance, Dreamy dance, Dreamy dance." They clapped in time to their shouts, and stamped their feet.

"Okay, boys, okay." Dreamy spoke to Mischa who walked over to the piano. Together they sorted through the music. "I'll be back in a few minutes."

The men kept up their shouting and stamping until she reappeared. They were suddenly hushed. She had changed from her long sequined dress into an almost transparent lace gown. Whistles and shouts of approval welcomed her. She signalled for silence. Mischa began to play. The music was slinky, seductive.

Dreamy danced. The men watched. It wasn't until they saw the long dress slip to the floor, that they realised what sort of a dance this was going to be. There were shouts of encouragement. Igor watched with his mouth open. Rhodes hurriedly adjusted his wig and took a reassuring pull at his hooch.

Dreamy slowly reached down and caressed Hennessey's cheek. She sat on his lap and nibbled his ear. Then she raised one of her sleek legs and seductively rolled down the stocking. She draped it around the coloured sergeant's neck. "Oh, man," he groaned.

She stood, sauntered over to Collins, put her foot on his

knee and smoothed down the second nylon. Collins's glasses steamed over. He removed them and polished them frantically on the table cloth. But by the time he'd got them on again, she was at the other side of the room, unzipping the back of her shiny silk bodice as she went. She shrugged her way out of it, slowly. Now she was wearing just panties and bra.

"Take 'em off," chanted the Marines. "Take 'em off." The noise was deafening. It was impossible to hear the music. She wriggled her shoulders and unclipped herself. With a slinky movement she spun off the bra. Only the smallest of stars covered her breasts. The noise grew even louder. As she took off her remaining garment, Morelli risked assassination—he killed the lights. In the dimness of the dying candles, both Dreamy and Morelli escaped.

Dreamy's Dive Bar had certainly had a gala inauguration.

15

The small tent of blanket just below Albert's stomach was a regular morning reminder. He'd awakened to it every day for the past week. He lay there and thought about it. A complex problem, he decided. Victoria was the cause—and his remedy. But how? Or, rather, where? There wasn't any privacy. He hadn't been really alone with her since the night of the Russian party. And he suspected he'd made a mess of that.

He was a millionaire unable to spend his money. And he had a would-be mistress he couldn't get at. He was frustrated. The money could wait, he thought, but his sex life couldn't. There HAD to be a way.

Albert sat up and lit a cigarette. He needed a plan. He looked across the cabin at Igor, still asleep on the opposite bunk. Below him he could hear Sacha snoring quietly. There was no point in smuggling her in here. Every crew member walked through this cabin to the lavatories. Rhodes or Collins were always around, so the tent was out of the question. Anyway, Dreamy was now in the neighbouring compartment.

The cave had been the only part of the Island that offered privacy. But since it'd become the distillery, it was guarded day and night. He'd thought of taking her out in a boat, but he knew that the safety-conscious Marines kept a binocular watch on the fishermen the whole time they were at sea.

He contemplated eloping. He decided there were too many drawbacks. They hadn't got passports, so they couldn't go abroad, and he couldn't draw his money quickly from his Zurich bank. They probably wouldn't even be allowed to land in Britain—because security was still being imposed. And he wasn't that sure he wanted to get married.

It was the lunchtime lobster thermidor that seeded the idea. It made him ill. He was sick. He knelt on the pebbly beach, retching into the sea. It was the one time he could have done without Victoria's company. But she came and sat next to him, and put her arm round his shoulder. She was sympathetic.

"Come and lie down in the tent for a while. I'll go and get Zeke."

The tall Kentuckian examined him, as Albert lay sweating and uncomfortable on Victoria's bed.

"You sure look sick," said Zeke. "An' blotchy. If Ah didn't know who cooked your meals, Ah'd think you'd been food poisoned."

The idea sprouted. Albert remembered a scene in The Indian Mutiny, where the entire garrison went down with cholera.

"No," lied Albert. "It's not what I've eaten. I've been feeling worse every day. I used to be an ambulance cadet. I think I've got . . ." He thought quickly. His idea blossomed. "I think I've got Jacob's Disease. It's a mild form of summer cholera. It's not fatal. It only lasts a few days. Dreadfully contagious. Have to be isolated right away. So should everyone else who's been in close contact with me."

Zeke stepped back. "Me, too?" he asked.

"No, you haven't been close enough."

"What's the treatment?"

"Just rest, and cold compresses on my head, day and night."

"Ah can do that," said Zeke.

"No, you might pass it on to the others with their food. It had better be someone who's already had contact with me and hasn't caught it. They might be immune." He paused. "Maybe Victoria?" He remembered a death scene in Beau Geste, and let his head loll sideways. Trying, at the same time, to make the white of his eyes show.

"Of course, I will," he heard Victoria say.

"Ah'll get a tent put up between the wire and the trawler," said Zeke. "It's as far away from anyone as we can get. Then Ah'll radio the fleet for instructions."

Albert was suddenly alert again. "No," he said. "You don't

176

need instructions. I know how to cure it. It's quite common where I come from. I've had it before . . . several times."

Zeke built the pup tent in a small depression between the rocks on the Russian side of the wire. Then he painted a notice—Isolation Ward—and pinned it to the canvas. Victoria made up a bed in the tent, then wrapped Albert carefully in a layer of blankets and led him over.

It was dark inside. Dark and private. Albert lay on his back looking up at the kneeling Victoria. He was a model invalid. He groaned. She pressed a damp cloth to his forehead. He was weakly appreciative. He held her hand and coughed consumptively. He tried foaming at the mouth but it wasn't obvious enough in the darkness. His delirious rambling was much more convincing, he thought. He couldn't see the expression on Victoria's face, but he could tell by her voice that she was anxious. He felt guilty and decided to improve his condition slightly.

By evening, he was beginning to find some weaknesses in his plan. He was bursting to go to the latrines. Victoria wouldn't leave him for a minute.

"I must go out," he croaked.

"Yes, darling," said Victoria. He knew she was humouring him.

"Going to be sick again," wheezed Albert, clutching his throat.

"Use this." Victoria stood a plastic bucket by his side.

"Need drinking water."

She held a cup for him to drink. Albert tried to think of something that she wouldn't already have with her. But Victoria's preparation for her vigil was faultless. She seemed to have everything.

"Cigar," he said, desperately.

"I'll light you a cigarette. You never smoke cigars."

Albert seized his one chance. "Must have a cigar. Got to have one. Need it to fumigate the tent."

"I'll get you one," said Victoria. She crawled out through the flap. Albert wriggled out the other end, and knelt in the darkness. He breathed a relieved sigh. He was back in the tent, choosing his next symptom, from an assortment of rehearsed convulsions, when Victoria returned. She lit the cigar and put it between his lips.

177

"I really needed that," he twitched.

Zeke brought over their food. Sandwiches for Victoria, a bowl of carefully prepared gruel for Albert. His stomach was still queasy from the lobster. As the evening passed, he decided that it was now time to tell Victoria the truth, so that they could spend their first night alone together.

"I feel fine now," said Albert.

"Yes, dear."

"Really. I feel perfect."

He tried to pull her down. She refused to move. She leant over and kissed him lightly. That was all.

"Come here," he said.

"Just try to sleep, darling."

"I don't want to sleep. I'm fine," he persisted. "Let me love you."

Victoria reached for the damp compress and held it to his forehead. "Just relax."

Albert pushed it away. "Dammit. I'm really fine. Now we're alone, can't we make love?"

"You're making yourself worse," said Victoria. "Just lie back and try to rest. You're breathing too quickly. If I leave you alone, will you be good? I just want to get my night things and then I'll be back."

Albert promised. At least, she was going to spend the night with him. There'd be opportunity enough later. She was back a few minutes later in her dressing gown, with two cups of hot chocolate.

"Try to drink this. It'll make you feel better."

Albert gulped down half the mug. "I invented Jacob's Disease. He's the bloke in the Bible who had to send to Egypt for his oats. I was beginning to feel like him."

Victoria smiled.

Albert played his trump card. "I love you," he said.

Victoria kissed him. "And I love you, darling." He tried to unfasten her dressing gown.

"Now just relax," she whispered. "You'll feel fine tomorrow. Zeke's put a sleeping draught in your drink."

"No! Oh, no!" He just had time to moan the words before the tent started to spin . . .

As Albert swirled into his coma, it was late afternoon in

New York. The United Nations' Building threw a long shadow that brought early dusk to the streets below. The home-bound New Yorkers fought through the congested sidewalks and plunged into the Subways. But, in the Security Council, work was far from ended.

"Aggression, aggression, aggression," shouted an Arab. He was screaming the words. He wasn't heard above the stamping and thumping and crashing of thirty other delegates who, unknown to each other, were agreeing with him.

Another hundred delegates also shouted, screamed, crashed, thumped and stamped. They didn't agree. It was business as usual.

Twenty grim, silent representatives were trying to filter the American UN Ambassador's speech through the noise. His interrupted words reached them, via the translators, over the earphones.

At the Russian table, a crop-haired man stood and turned to face the commotion. He held up his arms. The screaming Arab official became silent. The rest followed, awaiting the worded wisdom to come. The Russian eyed the Arab coldly. "If you and the other gentlemen keep quiet, you will allow the United States and the Soviet Union to make war in peace."

The twenty grim delegates clapped.

The British representative took advantage of the silence to lean along his table. He hissed past a junior to his colleague at the other end. "Psst." Lord D'Elpus turned towards him. "What's a five letter word, beginning with C that means to behave like a politician?"

An American spoke over his shoulder. "Try creep, bud."

The Briton ignored him. He wrote charm. But the rest of the crossword wouldn't work.

The American delegate continued: "We have not invaded. We have not provoked. We have not violated. We are the right and lawful protectors of our own territory. Our 51st State." He paused and rested forward on his hands. He looked tired.

"We want peace. But we will not tolerate, in any circumstances, any encroachment onto our soil, or rock, by Soviet or other non-Nato troops. No force will violate our territorial rights without the direst consequences." He sat down.

179

The Russian reply was immediate.

"The peoples of the Soviet Republic do not encroach. We claim only that to which we are legally and morally entitled. We have sought peace throughout these negotiations. In return, we are offered invasion, massacre, desolation. What has happened to the original inhabitants of Foul Rock? Where are they? Let me tell you all. They are not in Britain. They are not on the Continent. They are imprisoned in the American sector of the Island." He thumped his table.

"We will fight for their freedom. For the freedom of this, the smallest of the Russian States. For its people's freedom. The Americans claim they did not invade the territory. Yet they were not there when the Soviet base was established. They landed a massive armed Naval force long after the Island's people had appealed to us to adopt their territory. The Island was economically in an unhappy state. It was in need of Soviet aid." He took a long swig from the water glass in front of him.

"There are no imprisoned inhabitants in the Soviet territory of Foul Rock. For years, the American aggressors have threatened the Soviet peoples. This is, as they say themselves, the end of the line. We will not be pushed further. Unless all American troops are withdrawn from Foul Rock within one week, we will take whatever action is necessary to remove them." The Russian pulled his handkerchief from his pocket, and wiped a sweating forehead. Before he could continue, the American delegate burst in.

"This is an unprovoked threat of hostility. Foul Rock is US territory. We hold the deeds—as examined by the Secretary-General, and by the Soviet delegation. But we are in no way intimidated by Soviet war talk. As the most powerful nation on earth we are pledged to defend Foul Rock, as we would protect California, or Alaska." He looked menacingly at the Russians.

"America will not be the first to declare war, but we will punish severely any nation who forces us into armed conflict."

The argument was still continuing when Albert awoke the next morning.

Albert was obviously well. Victoria smiled happily when

180

he propped himself up on his elbow to drink the tea she'd brought him. His plan had backfired, but he couldn't really blame her. And there was still tonight to look forward to.

"I think I'm quite well, now," said Albert.

"You look a lot better."

"I meant what I said last night." He was surprised with himself. He really did mean it. "I love you."

"And I meant what I said." Victoria kissed him.

"We'll be alone tonight," said Albert. "For the first time, really alone."

Victoria kissed him again.

The fishing parties were out early, but it was Hennessey's unusual prize that caught the interest that morning. He stood, surrounded by a crowd. They were looking at the huge, banjo-shaped monkfish draped over the rocks by the jetty.

"Jees, it must weigh a hundred pounds," said Morelli. He was sucking the earpiece of his transistor radio.

"Better get your flies fastened, Macaroni. It's still alive," said Zeke, eyeing the battery of teeth.

"What do I do? Eat it, or play it?" queried Hennessey.

"Him no good. Taste like wool blanket," advised Boris. "Only good for throw away or maybe lobster pot bait."

Ace clubbed the fish with Igor's harpoon, and the men cut it into strips and rebaited the lobster pots.

By mid-day, the sun was too hot, even for fishing. The men spent the hottest part of the afternoon lying in the shade of the missile launcher or wallowing like sleek, brown seals in the water at the edge of the rock. It was a relief when the sun began to drop.

Now there was no way of telling the American Marines from the Russian seamen. They dressed alike, mostly in slacks or swimming shorts, and sat around in intermingled groups. The men rested and lived where they chose. Russians in the American camp. Americans in the shade of the *Dmitri Kirov* or the cool of the cabins below decks.

They were no longer Russian or American—they were Foul Rock Islanders.

Evening brought a crisis. There was something wrong with the still. The men stood around in the distillery cave, holding a gloomy inquest. During the day the still's output had dropped. By tea-time it had slowed to a trickle. By early evening it had stopped altogether.

"Temperature's too low," said Ushakov. "Something's happened to the gas flow."

They looked under the tarnished copper at the flame below. It glowed a weak blue and shimmered just above the rocks. Ushakov held his hand in it.

"Not hot enough to boil the mash."

The heat of the flame for the past few weeks seemed to have powdered the rocks around the outlet. Splinters had fallen down the fissure.

"I think it's blocked," said Ushakov. "Perhaps it will be difficult to free."

"Maybe we can rig up a gasoline burner," said Hennessey. "It shouldn't be too difficult."

"Yes," agreed Vorolokov. "But I think we can maybe clear blockage. If we can hit with long rod, maybe we can move stone."

They dismantled the heavy boiler and dragged it clear of the gas hole, then smothered the flame with a piece of wet burlap. Poking down the bore with lengths of aluminium tubing from Rhodes's frame tent didn't help. Whatever was blocking the hole stayed solidly in place some fifteen feet below the surface. Short of actually excavating the area, there was nothing to be done.

"It must have to be a gasoline burner," said Ushakov to Hennessey. "How long will it take build one?"

"I guess we can make one in a couple of days," said Hennessey. "The trouble is that we're going to start using a lot of juice, and it's not going to be too safe."

"Maybe we should use driftwood," said Corrigan. "Less dangerous."

"Not enough," said Vorolokov. "Anyway, too late today. Must now leave until tomorrow. Not good, with night club, we get short of hooch."

"We'll have to go back on rations tonight," said Corrigan.

Igor stood watching and listening, a sad expression on his face. Suddenly, he looked cheerful. He knew a way to clear the blockage. He turned and hurried out of the cave.

Albert's day was tedious. His miniature blanket tent had lasted longer than usual. He hid it from Victoria by tucking the tent pole into his pyjama belt. It subsided only when he had a succession of noisy visitors, all of whom stood well away from the tent doorway and talked to him. Although both he and Victoria knew his sickness had passed, he kept the symptoms whenever the guests appeared.

By mid afternoon, the blanket tent returned with refreshed anticipation. By evening, it was an unsatisfied ache.

"They're having trouble with the still," said Victoria. "The gas supply seems to have stopped. They're going to make a petrol burner. We're back on rations tonight. Daddy's furious He said it was gross neglect. It'll do him good to go without."

"I hope you don't think that it does me good to go without," said Albert.

"I didn't think you were that fond of hooch."

"Who's talking about hooch. I love you. Come to bed."

"Later, when they've turned in."

It wasn't long before the activity of the Island died, but to Albert it seemed like another day. From the tent, they could hear the singing in the night club. Dreamy wasn't stripping. "Special occasions only," she said.

She sang, the men drank. She even rationed the singing, and Boris and Zeke rationed the hooch.

At last, Albert and Victoria heard the men clambering their way down the rope ladder and stumbling across the rocks towards the tents. There were a few shouted good nights, a couple of ribald comments, and then the sea-scarred silence of an island at night—the soft swish of the waves, and the chatter of the pebbles. The night was warm. There was no moon, but the sky was freckled with stars.

Albert unfastened the end of the tent above his head and stared up. "Millions and millions," he said.

"You mean your money?"

"No, the stars. Come and look."

Victoria slid down alongside him. He pointed upwards. "Look, Orion. And the Seven Sisters."

"And The Plough, and the Nor ..." Albert's mouth cut her off in mid-sentence. He pulled the flap of the tent closed.

"Get undressed," he whispered.

"No," said Victoria.

"Why?"

"Because I want you to undress me." Victoria was shivering.

Albert stroked her cheek.

"You're crying," he said, surprised.

"Yes, a little. It's because I want you." Victoria's body throbbed. She could feel her blood thumping through the veins at her temples. Her body felt exposed, although she was still dressed. Albert rolled towards her. His leg pushed between hers. She could feel his tensed thigh pressing against her.

"Undress me."

His hands fumbled. She was glad he was gentle. Albert untied the bow at the waist of her dress and half-lifted her. He slid the material down. She kicked it away. He could feel the softness of the skin over her ribs. Her bra was silky above it. He kissed her shoulders. She whimpered. He pushed the bra straps off her arms and unclipped the back. It fell away.

Albert ran his tongue down the hollow between her breasts, then pulled her towards him, until he could trace a course around them, then to her neck and ear. He blew softly. She shuddered.

Albert was a maestro. A sexual virtuoso. He caressed a symphony. He drew Victoria towards an inevitable crescendo, as artistically as a Liszt rhapsody. Albert frequently envied his film heroes. Had they known of his ability, they would have envied him.

Victoria ran her fingers through the hair on Albert's chest. Men liked that, the Kama Sutra said. He was already naked beneath the blanket. She tugged it away from him.

Albert slid his hand, palm flat against her stomach, under the elastic of her nylon briefs. She shivered again, then lifted herself so that he could ease them off. He ran his fingers along her thigh. His tongue traced downwards. He felt the muscles of her stomach tremble.

"I love you," he told her.

"Be kind. You'll hurt me," she whispered.

He could feel the warm welcome of her body. Her

clenched hands tightened. Her nails dug into him. He winced. The pressure relaxed.

A slim, dark figure darted from the trawler towards the unguarded hooch cave. It ran lightly over the rocks and skirted the seaweed dark pools. It stood for a second above the cave and looked around, then it dropped out of sight.

Igor pulled aside the flap across the entrance. The cave was, as he had hoped, unguarded. The light, with its wire to the trawler's generator, silhouetted him as he stood in the entrance. He stepped in.

He stood for a while, looking down at the blocked gas outlet, then pulled an empty Coca-Cola tin from a pocket. From another, he drew a grenade, and a spool of fishing line. He punched a hole in the bottom of the can with his knife, and threaded the cord through, knotting it inside. Then, with great care, he pushed the grenade into the tin so that the sides gripped the lever. Then he pulled out the pin.

Slowly, he lowered the primed bomb, on the fishing line, down the gas fissure. The pressure of the spring-loaded lever against the inverted tin would hold the grenade safely in place. It slipped a fraction. Igor shut his eyes. It held. He wiped a hand across his forehead, then continued lowering the charge down the outlet until he felt it stop against the obstruction.

"My love," breathed Victoria. She could feel Albert, burning, against her.

"You'll have to help, darling," said Albert quietly.

"How?" asked Victoria, completely forgetting a full term's dormitory study of the Hindu sex manual.

"Like this." He took her hand.

Albert pressed himself forward again. Victoria's nails scored his back.

Igor retreated from the cave, paying out the line as he went. He stood a few yards away, to one side of the entrance Then he jerked the line, suddenly, and clasped his hands over his ears. Nothing happened. He waited a moment. Then jerked the cord even more fiercely. This time, the tin came bouncing out of the cavern—empty. There was silence for a few seconds. Then, to Igor, the world erupted.

"Now, darling, now." Victoria's voice was urgent.

She saw a bright orange flash of light. The ground shook. "Albert," she gasped.

The tent disappeared. She saw the stars above them. Then there was a shattering explosion. A cathedral of flame leapt upwards with the roar of a thousand steam locomotives.

Albert jerked suddenly, and sagged. Something warm and sticky dripped from his head onto Victoria's face. It ran down to her lips. It was salty. She spluttered. It was blood. In panic, she pushed Albert aside. He slumped onto the mattress. The jetting flame lit the Island like a monster blow-torch. She could see blood pumping from a long cut on the side of his face.

"Daddy," she screamed. The Island was awake. She pulled the blanket around herself like a toga. Rhodes was at her side. He wasted no time. Sober and efficient, he felt carefully for a pressure point to stop the bleeding. Then he tore a strip off the sheet and pressed a pad on Albert's wound.

"Get Zeke," he ordered.

Victoria ran in the direction of a crowd of Marines looking up at the flame.

"Fall in. Fall in," shouted Corrigan. The Grunts ran to the parade ground. "Get a roll call," bellowed the Major. "Find out if everyone's here."

Hennessey obeyed.

"All correct, sir, except for Zeke. He's got a wounded man over there." He pointed to where Albert's pup tent had stood.

The Russians were collecting below the side of the trawler. It glowed, looking red-hot in the strange light. Vorolokov ran over.

"We're short of Igor," he called to Corrigan. "Is he with you?"

"No. Hennessey, take Morelli and see if you can find Igor."

"Sir." The dark top-sergeant grabbed Morelli by the arm and they doubled round the back of the tents.

"What's happened?" asked Vorolokov.

"Don't know," replied the Major. "It looks like we've got a volcano on our hands. Can we get it out?"

"Doubt it. Cannot get so near enough to do anything."

Even as they spoke, there was another explosion. A large piece of Island detached itself and soared out into the sea. The men ducked as smaller pieces scattered over the rocks.

The blast of hot air burnt the front of Hennessey's crinkly black hair as he and Morelli turned the corner of the Mess hut. He covered his eyes with his hands and ducked back behind the shelter.

"You okay, Sarge?" Morelli was shouting to make himself heard above the hissing roar.

"Yep. See him anywhere?" Hennessey rubbed his hand over his forehead and the stumpy bristle where he was now burnt bald.

Morelli peered carefully round the corner of the hut.

"I think he's down there. It looks like there's a body in the pool by the cave. May be dead."

"We got to get him."

"We'll have to pass by the flame. It'll cook us."

Their eardrums throbbed with the sub-sonic vibrations.

"Swim round," shouted Hennessey. He pointed towards the beach.

They ran down into the water and waded out until they were able to duck beneath the waves. The contrast between the extreme heat and cold sea made them gasp.

They stumbled, half-swam through the waist deep water, until they were within a few yards of the flame and Igor's still body. He lay in a small rock pool, his head on a clump of weed. His clothes were smouldering.

Hennessey shouted again. Morelli could see his mouth moving. He couldn't hear him. The Sergeant stumbled out of the water and dashed towards Igor. Morelli followed. The heat scorched them. They dived into the pool next to Igor. The water was steaming.

Hennessey pointed back at the sea. They grabbed the young Cossack by his arms and legs and dragged him with them. The blast of another explosion threw them the remaining few feet into the water. Morelli floundered. His hands stung. He looked down at them—they were skinless.

187

Eyes wide, he stared at Hennessey as the bulky Sergeant grabbed at the unconscious Russian. Hennessey's face was visibly peeling.

He waved vaguely away from the flame. The two Marines ducked down into the water, towing Igor between them.

"They've got Igor," shouted Suki. Two blackened figures stumbled over the steaming rocks, dragging a limp body between them. "They're hurt."

Corrigan and his Grunts ran towards them. The Major sucked in his breath as he saw the singed faces and hands of his two men.

"Get 'em to the other side of the Island," he shouted to Suki. "Get Zeke, if he's free. They need attention badly."

There was another explosion.

"Ace, get those missiles dumped in the sea," shouted Corrigan. "Then prepare to abandon ship."

Corrigan ran towards Hennessey and Morelli. He grabbed Igor's feet and lifted him from the ground.

"Hit the boats," he yelled to Ace. "Count everyone in. And don't forget the Limeys. Vorolokov, better get your men afloat." The Major hoisted Igor onto his shoulders and almost ran with him over the rocks to the Marines' boats.

Ushakov appeared through the smoke, his arm held over his head as protection against the falling rocks. "Corrigan, Corrigan." He grabbed the sweating Major by the arm. "Have you radio fleet?"

The Major looked at Clancy, who was working over the set.

"Sorry, it's dead, sir."

"Quick, give me wavelength. Must send message. Stop war." The scientist was agitated.

"What d'you mean?"

"Soviet Fleet thought you attack us, blow up Island. We explained only natural explosion. They not attack now. But your people must be warned."

"Let me get at your radio," gasped Corrigan. "Clancy, come with us."

The three men ran back to the trawler.

Minutes later, as the Island grumbled and quivered, Corrigan and Clancy Paradise made the beach.

"Everyone's in the boats, sir," reported Hennessey. He

spoke with his jaw stiff. His lips were split and bleeding. "All present and correct. Two Russians as well. Boris and Igor. Igor's still out. Burns, a broken arm and maybe some ribs. Albert's got a bad wound on his head, but he'll be okay."

"Push off," shouted Corrigan. His words were almost lost in a further explosion which chipped off another large hunk of the Island. Foul Rock trembled and shook so much that it radiated small tidal waves that threatened to swamp the boats. "Push off. Get clear and stay together."

The outboard engines started. They were barely audible above the roar of the flame. The boats pulled away. The sea was splashed with orange, the light strong enough to see the Russians motoring clear of the curtain of rock shrapnel.

Albert felt nothing of his injuries, although he was half-conscious as Zeke worked on him. He watched the soaring flame, and felt the powdered rock falling in a fine dust on his face and shoulders. He remembered The Last Days of Pompeii. He stood, a silent, brave Roman soldier, at his post to the last. The lava crept nearer. A blizzard of hot ashes sifted through the columned portals and gathered around his ankles. He was being buried alive. It gave him some satisfaction to know that he would be excavated eventually ... to become immortalised in a painting, a book. AND a film.

The American and Russian boats drew together half a mile away from the diminishing Island.

"Amazing," called Vorolokov. "Never before have I seen such. What happened?"

"Maybe a flashback down the outlet to the gas pocket. Sort of volcano, I guess."

"Is your comrades all right?"

"Four casualties," replied Corrigan. "Igor and Albert are hurt, not very seriously. Igor's got a broken arm and ribs, Albert concussion, and Hennessey and Morelli got burnt. The fleet should be here tomorrow. Dreamy's giving Igor medical treatment. Are the rest of your crew okay?"

"All men and dog are rescued."

Zeke and Boris were whispering together in the bow of the second boat.

189

"That restaurant idea we had. Ah've only a month left to serve. Ah'm too old to make another stretch. Ah'll have a pretty good pension. How about it?"

"Truly?" asked Boris.

"Yup," answered Zeke gruffly. 'Ah reckon we could make good business. Fifty-fifty partnership. Want me to ask?"

"What about Igor? Him is like my son."

"Igor, too."

"Yes, ask pliss."

"Major," called Zeke. "It's important, can we come along-side?" They steered the boat until it rubbed against the Major's launch. "Boris and Igor want to stay with us." He explained their idea.

Corrigan rubbed his chin. "You hear that, Vorolokov?" he called to the Russian boat. "Boris and Zeke want to open a restaurant in France."

"We hear it."

"What do you think? Do you agree?"

"Agree to what?" asked Vorolokov.

"To Boris and Igor staying with Zeke."

"Sad about Boris and Igor," said Vorolokov gravely. He looked around his crew. "Heroes they died when Island exploded. A great sadness. If they living, we all want wish them much good luck and happiness." Vorolokov stood, his arm round Tanya's shoulders, smiling across at the Americans.

A crackling series of eruptions behind them made them look towards the Island. There was little left now. The hull of the *Dmitri Kirov* shone golden, like a burial ship, in the geyser of light. They watched the bow tilt sharply upwards. There was another explosion. The trawler slipped towards the sea and relaunched herself. For a moment she looked as though she would float. Then, stern-first she slid under the waves. There was a final explosion that blew the Island to pieces. A roar of bubbling gas and then silence. The flame died. The night was black.

For a while no one spoke.

"How will you get back," Corrigan called across the widening gap to the Russian boat.

"We're fishermen," came Ushakov the scientist's proud reply. "We'll manage until the supply ship picks us up."

190

The boats drifted farther apart.

Albert was leaning back against the hard thwart of the boat, his head cradled by Victoria. He'd watched the destruction of his Kingdom without comment. Now he sat up and shouted to the disappearing Russians.

"Good luck, Captain Vorolokov. And thanks."

The Russian's reply was drowned by an argument between Boris and Zeke.

"We'll call it the Old Kentucky."

"Niet. The Moscovite Restaurant."

"The Moscovite Kentuckian," compromised Zeke.

"Da," said Boris. "The Moscovite Kentuckian it will be. And such lovely borsch we will serve, with sweet corn and ketchup."

"And Igor will be special dancing for peoples at night," said a weak voice from the bottom of the boat. "Attracting most everybodies."

"That'll cost you your pension in crockery," said Morelli. The two boatloads of Marines laughed.

"Not much to show for my Island." Albert's voice was sad.

"Only three million quid," Gin Jim Rhodes reminded him.

"And this," said Victoria. "It's what laid you out."

She handed him a sharp piece of limestone—the sole surviving remnant of the Island won by Uncle Alf, off Fatty Hagan, in a poker game.